£895/ £299

From a nameless, homeless and hungry tramp of the roads to a well-dressed heir of vast estates and a baronetcy.

It was a lucky break for Ragged Dick when Fate brought him and Sir Henry Compton together. But it had its drawbacks, as the former tramp discovered when he went to Greyfriars and found himself under Bunter's thumb – and subject to the bitter malevolence of a rascally relative.

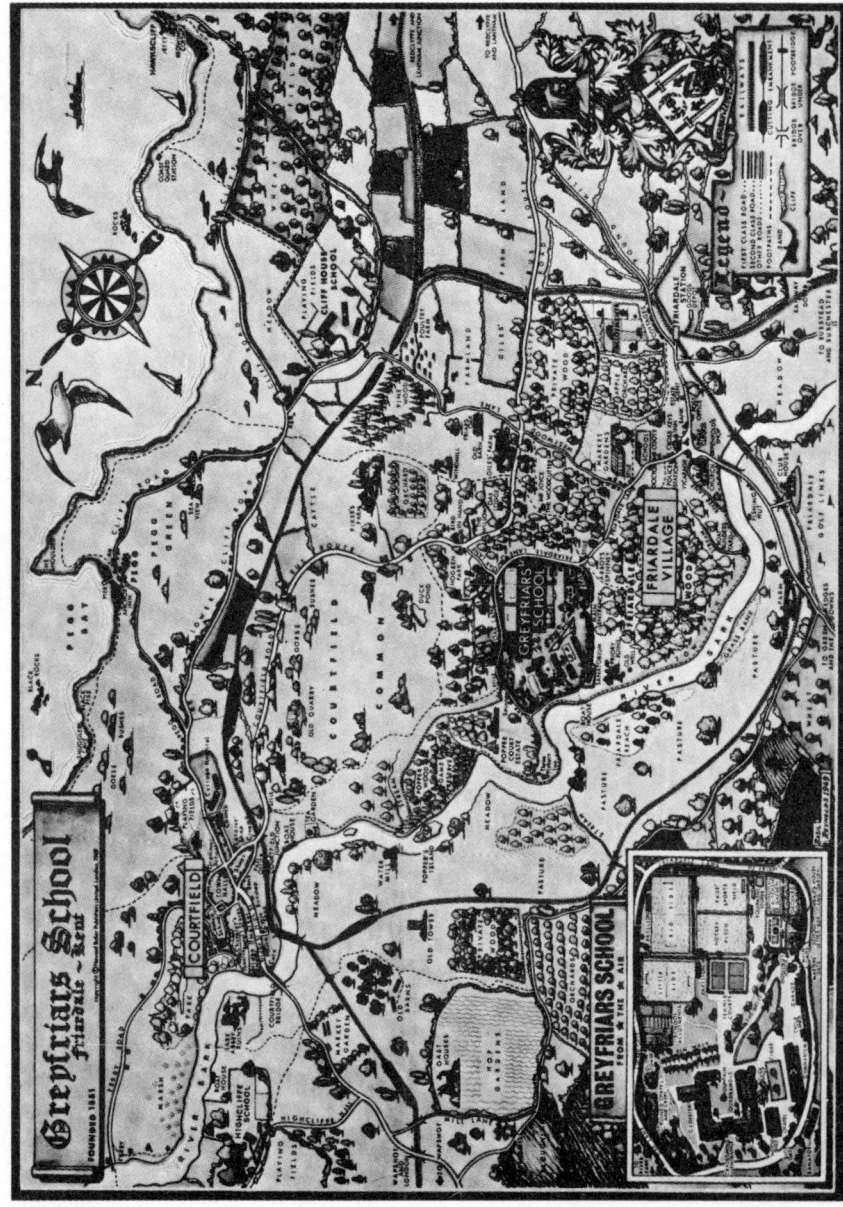

BILLY BUNTER'S TRAMP

BILLY BUNTER'S TRAMP

by
Frank Richards

HOWARD BAKER
LONDON

BILLY BUNTER'S TRAMP!

Frank Richards

© Copyright HOWARD BAKER PRESS LIMITED 1979
S.O.L. 253 © The Amalgamated Press Ltd., 1935

ISBN : 0 7030 0177 9

A HOWARD BAKER BOOK

Greyfriars Press Books are published by
Howard Baker Press Ltd.,
27a Arterberry Road, Wimbledon, London SW20
Typesetting by Triste Ltd., Croydon, Surrey.
Printed in Great Britain by
A. Wheaton & Co. Ltd., Exeter.

CONTENTS

CHAPTER

CHAPTER 1

Bunter, Too!

"**W**AITING for you!" said Billy Bunter.

"Eh?"

"Ready at last — what?" asked Bunter affably.

The Owl of the Remove detached his fat figure from the old stone gateway of Greyfriars School as Harry Wharton & Co. came along.

He blinked at the Famous Five with a cheery grin.

Bunter seemed to be glad to see the chums of the Remove. But the gladness seemed to be all on his side.

"Hallo, hallo, hallo! What are you waiting for?" inquired Bob Cherry.

"For you, old fellow," said Bunter affectionately. "You didn't think I'd desert an old pal on a half-holiday, did you?"

"No — only hoped so," answered Bob.

"Oh, really, Cherry — "

"Roll away, fatty!" said Johnny Bull. "We're going for a jolly long tramp, and you'd crock up after the first mile."

"I suppose I'm as good a walker as any fellow here," said Bunter, with a sniff. "It's all right. I'm coming."

"Don't be an ass, old man," said Harry Wharton. "We're going as far as Compton Woods, up the coast. That's a good six miles, and rough going most of the way."

"Why not have it in Friardale Wood?"

"Eh? Have what?"

"The picnic," said Bunter.

Bunter's eye was on a little bundle that Bob Cherry carried slung over his arm.

The Owl of the Remove, as usual, was after the loaves and fishes. Evidently it was not the fascinating society of the Famous Five that attracted him.

"What's the good of walking that distance?" argued Bunter. "Sheer waste of time. Now, if you have the picnic in Friardale Wood, you can have a nap under the trees afterwards, instead of a long walk home. See? Ever so much better."

Bob Cherry chuckled.

"But we're not going out for an afternoon nap," he explained. "We're going out for fresh air and exercise."

"What utter rot!"

"Every chap to his opinion!" assented Bob cheerfully. "Goodbye, Bunter! Go and take a nap."

"Pleasant dreams!" grinned Nugent.

And the chums of the Remove walked out of the gates. They tramped away cheerily in the sunshine up Friardale Lane. There was a patter of feet on the road behind them.

"Hallo, hallo, hallo! Here comes Bunter!"

Bunter came up, panting.

"I say, you fellows, don't walk so fast, you know! Give a chap a chance!"

"Goodbye!" said Wharton.

"The fact is, Harry, old man, I want to have a look at Compton Woods," said Bunter. "I've been going there for a long time, only—only— "

"Only you were too lazy to walk the distance!" suggested Johnny Bull.

"The fact is, it's a jolly good idea to get some fresh exercise – I mean, some fresh air and exercise – on a half-holiday," said Bunter. "This idea of a walk to Compton Woods is simply tip-top. I'm glad you fellows thought of it."

"Ha, ha, ha!"

"It's really ripping!" said Bunter. "I shall enjoy it no end! Can I carry the parcel for you, Bob?"

"And do the vanishing-trick round the first corner?" grinned Bob. "No, thanks."

"Oh, really, Cherry! If you think I know there's a cake in that bundle, you're mistaken. I never looked into the study while you were packing it."

"Ha, ha, ha!"

"It's just the walk I want," said Bunter, trotting on cheerily, "and the society of you fellows, you know. I've turned down a lot of chaps to come out with you this afternoon."

"Turn 'em up again!" suggested Johnny Bull.

"Lord Mauleverer wanted me to go out in the car with him," went on Bunter. "He fairly begged me to go, but – "

"Does Mauly beg with his foot?" asked Frank Nugent.

"Eh?"

"I saw him kick you when you were hanging round the car."

"Ha, ha, ha!"

"The fact is, Mauly's a bit of a bore," said Bunter. "I decided not to go, after – "

"After he kicked you?"

"No, you ass! After I found that you fellows were going for a walk. After all, you're one of my oldest pals at Greyfriars, Harry. You remember how I stood by you the first day you came?"

"I remember you borrowed half-a-crown the first day I came," answered the captain of the Remove.

"Oh, really, Wharton – "

"And I remember you never squared."

"The fact is, I was going to square that half-crown this very afternoon, Wharton – "

"Shell out, then!"

"Only I've been disappointed about a postal-order — "

"The same postal-order you had been disappointed about the day I came?" inquired Wharton.

"Ha, ha, ha!"

"No!" roared Bunter. "Another postal-order. I say, Bob, don't you find that bundle a little heavy?"

"A little," agreed Bob, shifting the bundle to his other arm.

"Let me carry it, old chap."

"It would soon grow lighter if Bunter carried it!" chuckled Nugent.

"The lightfulness would soon be terrific."

"I think I'll stick to it," grinned Bob. "Goodbye, Bunter! We're coming to the hill now."

"Think I can't walk up a hill?" snorted Bunter.

"Better chuck it before you crock up. The farther you go the longer the walk home, you know."

"Rats!"

"Stick it if you like," said Harry Wharton, laughing. "Mind, we're not stopping this side of Compton Woods, Bunter. If you get there alive, you're welcome to a whack in the tuck. But it's six miles."

"I could do sixteen."

"Oh, my hat! Stick it, then!"

And the Co. walked on cheerily, and Billy Bunter tramped after them laboriously, breathing in jerks. With the prospect of tuck before him, Bunter felt as though he could walk unnumbered miles. His fat little legs fairly twinkled to keep pace with the strides of the sturdy Removites. To Harry Wharton & Co. it was quite an interesting question whether Bunter would crock up after the first mile, or whether he would last out two. Two, they considered, was his limit.

But Bunter was in a resolute mood.

He was as impecunious as usual that afternoon, and as it was an hour since dinner, he was more than ready for another meal. Nobody had been willing to cash a postal-order which he was expecting by the next post, and at the school shop Mrs. Mimble sternly declined to supply tuck on tick. The Famous Five were his only resources, therefore, if he was to get anything to eat before tea-time.

So, after two miles had been covered, Bunter was still fagging along the dusty road, with perspiration streaming down his fat face, and his podgy cheeks growing redder and redder, till they rivalled in hue a freshly-boiled beetroot.

CHAPTER 2

Bunter's Luck!

" I SAY, you fellows – "

"Save your breath, old man!" advised Bob Cherry. "You'll need it for the other four miles."

"I–I say – "

Bunter gasped and halted. More than two miles had passed behind him; two hundred, it seemed to Bunter.

"Stop a minute, you chaps! Let a fellow get his breath!"

The chums of the Remove considerately stopped.

"We'll give you two minutes," said Harry Wharton.

"I say, I've got a proposition to make," said Bunter, leaning on a tree and dabbing his damp face with a handkerchief that needed washing. "Suppose we stop here for the picnic – "

"Bow-wow!"

"Let a fellow finish. Let's have this tuck for a snack on the way, you know, and I'll stand you a topping feed at Compton Hall."

"Eh?"

"That's the idea!" said Bunter, blinking at the chums of the Remove. "I've never happened to mention it before, but Sir Henry Compton is an–an old friend of my pater's, you know – "

"We don't know!" grinned Bob.

"Well, you know now I've told you!" snapped Bunter.
"Not at all. We don't know even now you've told us."
"Ha, ha, ha!"

"They were schoolfellows together at—at Eton!" said
Bunter. "I can tell you that Sir Henry will be delighted —
overjoyed, in fact – if I come in with a few friends. He—he
loves to have bright young faces round him."

"Ha, ha, ha!" roared the Famous Five.

Compton Hall was a good distance from Greyfriars, but
the juniors had heard of Sir Henry Compton – a great landowner, and reputed to be a rather crusty old gentleman. It
was said that he had been soured by the death of his only
son, who had been killed in a car accident, leaving a little boy
in delicate health to carry on the ancient name.

Local gossip told of the grandfather's anxiety about the
lad's health – not so much because of his affection for him,
according to the gossips, but because he was on the worst of
terms with a cousin who was the next heir to the title and
estates. What truth there might be in that tattle of the
countryside, the Greyfriars juniors neither knew or cared, but
they knew that Sir Henry was about the last man in Kent
to welcome an unexpected crowd of schoolboys in his
ancestral hall.

"I say, you fellows, there's nothing to cackle at!" howled
Bunter. "I suppose you can take a fellow's word?"

"Pile it on!" said Bob Cherry. "Make the most of your
two minutes, old fat man!"

"We'll have what you've got in that bundle for a snack
now," urged Bunter, "and then I'll use my influence with
Sir Henry to get you a jolly good feed at the Hall – what?"

"Time's up!" said Harry.

"I say, you fellows – "

"Trot's the word!"

"Oh, dear!" gasped Bunter.

The juniors tramped on cheerily, and Billy Bunter tramped

after them with lagging footsteps.

Apparently the Famous Five were not prepared to hand the picnic over to Bunter on the prospect of a glorious spread at Compton Hall, that prospect being a little too nebulous to satisfy them.

In fact, Bunter's "yarn" was even thinner than his yarns usually were, and had evidently been invented on the spot. Had he enjoyed the entree at Compton Hall, his visit there would certainly have been paid at a much earlier date. His acquaintance with the wealthy baronet was limited to a distant view of Sir Henry riding about the country lanes.

Billy Bunter gasped and panted, and puffed and blew, as he tramped on.

By this time he repented, from the bottom of his podgy heart, that he had joined in the excursion at all.

Every mile seemed at least a league now, and the distance to Compton Woods simply illimitable.

But Bunter kept on.

It was as far back to Greyfriars now as to the woods that looked over the sea near Compton Hall, so it was useless to turn back. Having come so far, Bunter was determined to be in at the death.

"Only a mile now!" said Bob Cherry encouragingly, as the juniors entered a deep, shady lane, along which ran park palings for a great distance.

"That's Compton Park," said Frank Nugent. "There's the gates, Bunter, if you'd like to drop in and see Sir Henry."

Bunter snorted.

"I say, you fellows, let's stop here, and — "

"And call on the giddy baronet?" asked Bob, with a chuckle.

"Nunno! On second thoughts, I'd rather stick to you chaps. I'm not keen on grandeur and all that; I have enough of that at home at Bunter Court," said the Owl of the Remove, "I'd rather camp down by the roadside here, and—and— "

"Ha, ha, ha!"

"My hat! This jolly old bundle is getting heavy," remarked Johnny Bull.

The bundle had changed hands during the walk, all the five taking charge of it in turn. Johnny Bull was the present bearer.

"Let Bunter take a turn with it," said Frank. "We can keep an eye on him."

"Good egg!" said Bob. "There's no turning here; these palings keep right on to the woods we're going to. Bunter can't dodge away with it — "

"Oh, really, Cherry — "

"Here you are, Bunter!"

"Yah!"

Bunter made no movement to take the bundle now.

Under the eyes of the Famous Five he could not venture to open it and devour the contents, and there was no escape for him if he scudded off with it. One side of the lane was bounded by the high park palings, the other by a thick hawthorn hedge and ploughed fields. So Bunter's desire to carry the parcel had quite departed from him.

But the circumstances which made him unwilling to take his share of the burden make the Famous Five willing that he should take it.

"Carry it yourself, and be blowed!" said Bunter sulkily.

"Right-ho! But he that will not work, neither shall he eat!" grinned Bob Cherry. "Put on speed, you chaps. Bunter's tired of our company."

"I say, you fellows!" howled Bunter. "Hold on! I'll carry the bundle. I'm keen on it! I — "

"Ha, ha, ha!"

"Buck up, then, fatty!"

William George Bunter sulkily took the bundle, and tramped on with it on his fat shoulder savagely.

"Hallo, hallo, hallo!" exclaimed Bob Cherry suddenly. "What's the game? Look at that!"

BILLY BUNTER'S TRAMP!

The Famous Five halted. Bunter, only too glad to halt, leaned on the park palings, breathing hard, and dripping with perspiration. He did not even blink at the scene that had attracted the attention of the Famous Five. Through the clear, sunny air there had come a sharp, loud cry – a cry of pain, and by a gap in the hawthorn hedge Bob Cherry had seen what made him cut quickly across the lane and dash through the hedge, his chums following him fast.

Something evidently was going on in the field, but what it was was of no interest to the Owl of the Remove.

He blinked after the five juniors, and he was amazed and could scarcely believe in his good luck when he saw them vanish one after another through the gap in the hedge – forgetful of him, forgetful even of the bundle he carried.

Bunter's eyes gleamed.

He was tired, but he was not too tired for one more effort, if he had time. The chance was too good to be lost.

Like Moses of old, he looked this way and that way, but he realised that flight was in vain; he was not the man to win a foot-race, even with a good start.

Then he blinked at the park palings.

Here and there the ancient wood was cracked and broken, offering handhold and foothold to an active climber.

Billy Bunter was by no means an active climber, but he was spurred on by the dazzling prospect of enjoying that picnic all to himself, and leaving in the lurch the beasts who had made him walk five miles from Greyfriars.

His fat mind was made up at once.

With a swing of his arm, he hurled the bundle over the wall, and heard it drop among the ferns and bracken on the other side. Then he clambered desperately up.

Never had the Owl of the Remove exerted himself so swiftly and energetically. At every second he expected to hear the voices and the footsteps of the Removites on the road behind him.

He clambered with desperate speed, and reached the top of the palings, and rolled over, hanging by his fat hands on the inner side. Then he dropped, and landed with a grunt in a bed of ferns.

He sat there only a few moments to gasp for breath. Then he picked himself up, clutched up the precious bundle, and disappeared among the trees of Sir Henry Compton's park.

CHAPTER 3

Rough on a Ruffian!

"**O**H! Don't—don't!"

"You rotter!" shouted Bob Cherry.

He burst through the gap in the hedge.

On the inner side, on the strip of grass between the hawthorns and the ploughed field, there was a camp. Three sticks had been set up over a smouldering fire of hedgerow wood, and an iron pot swung there. By the hedge lay a sack and a bag, and some ragged articles of attire, which had apparently been washed in a pond and spread out to dry in the sun. A pedlar's pack lay near at hand, and there were two or three dirty utensils for eating and drinking. It looked like the camping-place of some tramp in hard luck.

There were two occupants of that camp — a man and a boy. The man, a thick-set, stubbly-faced fellow, whose face was hardened and coarsened by strong drink, held the boy in a savage grasp by the back of his collar, and with his free hand was laying on lashes with a thick strap. The blows rang almost like pistol-shots.

That was the sight that Bob Cherry had seen from the lane, and that had caused him to rush through the gap into the field.

The struggling boy looked as ragged and unkempt as the man who was beating him — anyone observing them

20

would have supposed that the two were a travelling pedlar and his son, from their looks. But from the savage way in which the pedlar was beating his victim, it could hardly have been supposed that he was the boy's father.

"Don't—don't! Oh, stop—stop!"

The boy seemed a sturdy enough fellow, but he was helpless in the muscular grasp of the tramp. He struggled in vain as the blows fell hard and heavy on his ragged back.

Bob Cherry did not stop to ask questions. The sight of the hapless lad struggling in the grasp of a ruffian, who was plainly the worse for drink, was enough for Bob.

He came scrambling through the hedge into the field, and pitched himself fairly at the ruffian.

Bob's grasp fastened on the lashing arm as it was falling again, and he wrenched at the man and fairly dragged him away from his victim.

The boy staggered and fell in the grass.

"Why — what — 'Oo the dickens — 'Ands off!" yelled the pedlar furiously, turning on Bob Cherry like a tiger.

"You cowardly rotter!" shouted Bob, his honest face blazing with anger. "How dare you pitch into a kid like that!"

"Pitch into him!" gasped the ruffian. "I'll pitch into you first, and 'im arter! I'll — "

He dropped the strap, and grasped Bob Cherry in both savage hands.

Sturdy and strong as Bob was, it would have fared badly with him had not his comrades been close at hand.

But the Co. were already there. As Bob reeled in the strong grasp of the pedlar they rushed into the fray and grasped the ruffian on all sides.

Bump!

The man came down on his back, his sprawling legs kicking away the smouldering camp-fire, and oversetting the iron-pot that swung from the upright sticks.

"Oh!" he roared. "Ow!"

"Sit on him!" gasped Bob.

Johnny Bull dropped heavily on the pedlar's chest. Bob Cherry secured his wrists and held on to them. And as the ruffian kicked and struggled, Hurree Jamset Ram Singh trod heavily on his legs.

The man gasped and spluttered, and a torrent of savage abuse poured from his mouth.

"Chuck that!" said Bob Cherry. "Shove a turf into his mouth if he doesn't chuck it!"

And as the ruffian continued to splutter out curses, Frank Nugent jerked a muddy turf from the ground and jammed it fairly into his mouth, after which the ruffian spluttered and gasped incoherently.

"That's better!" said Harry Wharton.

"The betterfulness is terrific!"

"Groogh! Hooch! Ooooogh!"

"Hallo, hallo, hallo! Stop, you young shaver!" shouted Bob Cherry.

The boy who had been rescued had picked himself up, and was darting away through the hedge.

"Stop!" called out Harry Wharton.

The boy did not heed.

Whether he supposed that hostility was intended towards him as well as towards his persecutor, or whether he was simply making the most of his opportunity to escape, the juniors could not know or guess. He vanished through the hedge with an active spring, and they heard the patter of his feet on the road as he fled.

"Young ass!" said Nugent.

"He's gone!"

"Well, I dare say he knows his own business best," said Harry Wharton. "If he wants to get away from this brute, we'll see that he has a good start."

"Yes, rather!"

The pedlar spluttered the mud from his mouth.

"You let a man go, young gents!" he panted. Finding himself helpless in the hands of five fellows, the ruffian had changed his tone very considerably. "Don't you let that boy get away!"

"Why not?" demanded Bob.

"He'll come to some 'arm," said the pedlar. "He's a bad lot, he is, and I was thrashing 'im for his good, I was."

"Well, if he's a worse lot than you are he must be a real corker!" said Bob Cherry. "You're more than half-drunk, you rotter, and I fancy that's why you were pitching into him."

"P'r'aps I've 'ad a drop," said the pedlar. "It's 'ot and dry work tramping the roads, an' I've 'ad 'ard luck. And that there Dick wouldn't fetch my dinner for me, so 'elp me!"

Wharton looked at him sharply.

"Where was he to fetch your dinner from?" he asked. "There isn't a shop within three or four miles of here."

The man scowled at him sulkily without answering. Wharton's brow darkened.

"You rotter! Do you mean that you wanted him to beg for you, or to steal something from the farm over yonder? You look like it!"

"You mind your own business!" snarled the pedlar. "It ain't any affair of yourn! Let me go!"

Johnny Bull settled himself more comfortably on the ruffian's broad chest.

"You're not going just yet," he said coolly. "If that kid wants to get clear of you, he's going to have a chance!"

"What-ho!" said Bob Cherry emphatically.

The juniors had had only a glimpse of the boy whom the ruffian spoke of as "Dick"; they had noticed only a dirty, dusty face and a suit of rags. What he might be like they did not know, but they could see what his persecutor was like. He was a dirty, brutal, hard-drinking ruffian, and it was pretty clear that his pedlar's pack was more or less of a pretence — an excuse for loafing about the roads and lanes, looking for chances of petty larceny. Whatsoever claim the man might have on the boy, it was pretty clear that the boy was better off without the companionship of such a character. It was clear, too, that Dick thought so himself, for he had disappeared promptly, and his footsteps had already died out of hearing.

"Who are you?" asked the captain of the Remove, eyeing the man as he wriggled in the grasp of the Greyfriars fellows.

"I'm Pedlar Parker," grunted the ruffian, "and that there boy belongs to me, he does!"

"Do you mean that you're his father?"

Pedlar Parker did not answer that question.

"Ten to one he isn't," said Bob. "The poor kid's a tramp, I should say. I wish he'd stayed and let us speak to him. Whatever he is, he's better off away from this brute."

"Yes, rather!"

"Will you let a bloke go?" muttered Parker, in tones of concentrated ferocity. "You'll only make it worse for Ragged Dick. I'll give him all the more to make up for this when I find him!"

"Ragged Dick!" repeated Wharton. "That is his name?"

"Name! That whelp hasn't got any name!" said Parker, with a savage jeer. "I picked him up under a hedge, and he's tramped with me for a few months, that's all. Saved him from starving, I did!"

"Yes; you look like a Good Samaritan — I don't think!" said Bob Cherry, in disgust. "Well, if you picked him up under a hedge, as you say, he has a right to clear off if he chooses."

"I'll make him suffer for it!"

"You won't have a chance," said Harry Wharton. "We'll jolly well see that you don't, you rotter!"

The man made a sudden savage effort, and almost threw off the juniors who were holding him. He rose to his knees, but the next moment he went down again with a crash.

"No, you don't!" grinned Bob Cherry.

"You young 'ound – "

"Give me that strap," said Bob. "I'll fix him."

"Here you are."

With the strap that had been used to beat the hapless Dick the pedlar's wrists were strapped together behind his back and the buckle secured. Then the juniors rose and left him sprawling in the grass.

"That'll keep you safe for a bit," said Bob Cherry, with a chuckle. "Now, if you swear any more you'll get some more mud in your mouth, so you'd better chuck it, see?"

Pedlar Parker scowled at him, and wrenched savagely at the strap. But it was a good strap, and it held him fast.

"We'll keep an eye on this Johnny for a bit," said Bob. "What about having the picnic here instead of going on to the woods? It would be only decent to give that kid a chance to get right away from that brute."

"Good!" said Harry. "Call Bunter. He's got the stuff."

"Hallo, hallo, hallo! Bunter!" roared Bob Cherry.

Bob's powerful voice rang far across the lane. Echo answered from a dozen directions, but answer of any other kind there came none.

"Bunter! Bunty! Bunter!" roared Bob.

"Is the silly ass deaf as well as silly?" growled Johnny Bull. "Better go and fetch him. I shouldn't wonder if he's started on the tuck."

Bob Cherry jumped back through the hedge into the road. There he stared round for Bunter.

But there was no sign of the Owl of the Remove. Billy Bunter had long vanished.

"Bunter!" bawled Bob Cherry.

"Can't you see him, Bob?"

"He's gone!"

"Gone! My hat!"

The junior's rushed into the road.

Bunter was gone, and the bundle was gone! There was no picnic, after all – or, rather, there was a picnic in some secluded and unknown spot, and William George Bunter was enjoying it all on his lonesome own. Harry Wharton & Co. stared up and down the solitary lane with feelings almost too deep for words.

"The–the–the awful villain!" gasped Bob at last. "He's bolted with the tuck!"

"My hat! I–I– " stuttered Wharton.

"After him!"

"Which way?" asked Nugent.

"Goodness knows!"

"Nothing doing," said Harry Wharton, after a pause. "I dare say he hasn't got far, but he will be pretty well hidden out of sight. We'll burst him for this!"

"The burstfulness will be terrific!" said Hurree Jamset Ram Singh. "But the grubfulness is off!"

"Oh, dear!"

"I'm jolly hungry!" said Bob.

"Same here!"

"Oh, the villain!"

"The toad!"

"The sweep!"

"The–the horrid burglar!"

In dismal mood the Famous Five went back into the field. After their walk they were ready for the picnic, but it was clear that there would be no tea till they got back to Greyfriars. Billy Bunter had been one too many for them.

Pedlar Parker scowled at them as they returned.

"Are you going to let me loose, blight you?" he said, between his discoloured teeth.

"Oh, you shut up!" growled Bob Cherry. "It's all your fault that we've lost our tuck, you rotter! Shut up, or you'll get my boot!"

And the tramp snarled and shut up.

The juniors sat down to rest and to discuss what was to be done. There was no picnic, and it was useless to keep on as far as Compton Woods; they would be famished by the time they arrived there, and there would be six miles to walk back to tea. They decided to rest a while — meantime keeping Pedlar Parker a prisoner — and then walk home; and they agreed that when they saw Bunter again they would make him feel that his fat life was not worth living.

Nugent, fortunately, had a packet of toffee in his pocket, and Bob had a bag of chocolates, and these extremely light refreshments were handed round and disposed of as they sat by the hedge, to an accompaniment of savage mutterings from Pedlar Parker. It was not till an hour had elapsed that the pedlar was released from his own strap, and the juniors turned their backs on him and started for Greyfriars.

By that time they had no doubt that Ragged Dick had placed a sufficient distance between himself and his enemy; and Pedlar Parker seemed to be of the same opinion, for instead of taking up a hopeless pursuit, he proceeded to rebuild his fire, and set up his pot again, muttering curses the while.

Harry Wharton & Co. walked on towards Greyfriars, giving little more thought to the ruffian or to the lad whom they had rescued from his brutality — at the cost of losing their picnic. They never expected to see either of them again, and little dreamed, just then, how, and in what strange circumstances they were to meet once more the tattered lad who bore the odd name of Ragged Dick.

CHAPTER 4

Bunter's Generosity!

" JUST the place!"

Billy Bunter blinked round cautiously.

Once within the walls of Compton Park, Bunter had remembered that old Sir Henry was "down" on trespassers, poachers, vagrants, and, indeed, all doubtful characters who should presume to come between the wind and his nobility. Any baronet ought to have been pleased to meet a Public school chap – a Greyfriars man, and especially such a fascinating fellow as Bunter – taking a stroll in his park. But from what Bunter had heard of Sir Henry Compton he did not expect that savage old gentleman to be pleased by such a meeting, if it occurred. And a keeper was only too likely to take Bunter by the scruff of his neck and run him out of the park, perhaps with a boot to help him out.

For which reasons Bunter realised it behoved him to be cautious. The park had offered a safe refuge from five "beasts" who would be certain to recapture that picnic if they could. But Bunter had no desire to fall out of the frying-pan into the fire. So his very spectacles gleamed with watchfulness as he stole through the park, dodging among the ancient trees which belonged to Sir Henry Compton, and which Sir Henry liked to keep wholly and solely to himself.

Now Bunter was at a good distance from the road, and

considered that he was safe from pursuit, even if the Famous Five guessed that he was in the park, and followed.

He halted by a little summer-house which stood among the trees. It had been a summer-house long ago, but was fallen into decay, overgrown with creepers, and almost crushed by drooping branches of oaks and elms. It was a secluded spot, and there was a rustic bench inside, and Bunter very much wanted to sit down.

So he pushed his way in through the tangle of creepers and sat on the old bench with a gasp of relief.

The place looked as if it was never visited, so wildly was it overgrown. But Bunter noticed several cigarette-ends in the grass, which looked as if someone sat there sometimes and smoked. However, there was no sign of anyone in the vicinity now, and Bunter felt safe.

Rapidly he unfastened the bundle.

His fat face glowed with satisfaction.

There were hard-boiled eggs and bread-and-butter and ham sandwiches and a bottle of lemonade and a cake – quite a large and fruity cake, and several other items.

That little feed had been intended for five, and there would have been enough for Harry Wharton & Co. And so there was very nearly enough for Bunter on his own.

Bunter, taken as a whole, was not an active fellow. But there was one part of Bunter accustomed to activity, inured to it by incessant exercise. That was his jaws. Eating was his favourite pastime, but talking came a good second. In one way or another Bunter's jaws were generally busy. Now they plunged into activity at an amazing rate. Probably, had Harry Wharton & Co. started all together on that spread the good things would not have disappeared as fast as they did now.

Item after item vanished, till only the cake remained. By that time even Bunter was slackening a little.

But he started cheefully on the cake. With so large a cargo already disposed of, it was slow work; but he did not mean to leave a crumb of it.

"This is good!" murmured Bunter.

Undoubtedly it was good. After the feast, doubtless there was the reckoning to come — when he had to face five enraged fellows at Greyfriars. But that was still in the future, and Bunter was not a fellow to meet troubles halfway. He dismissed Harry Wharton & Co. from his mind, and gave all his happy attention to the cake.

A footfall interrupted him.

He started, almost choking over the cake. He gave a startled blink at the overgrown entrance of the little shelter.

A strange figure appeared there.

It was that of a lad of about Bunter's own age, but of a very different build, and in very different attire. The face was dirty and dusty, to such an extent that it was a little difficult to see what the youth really looked like. But a close inspection would have shown that the features were good, the mouth well shaped, the eyes bright and clear and steadfast. The boy's clothing was simply rags and tatters — an old pair of trousers gaping with rents, a man's coat cut down and patched, a rag of a cap on the back of his untidy hair, a pair of worn-out boots, too large for his feet, through holes in which his grubby toes peeped.

Billy Bunter's startled glance changed to a stare of contempt.

He had dreaded to see a gaitered keeper, or the tall, formidable figure of Sir Henry Compton. This scarecrow had no terror for him.

He resumed munching his cake while he stared with blighting disdain at the "scarecrow."

The ragged youth had been about to enter the summerhouse, but he stopped half-way in at the sight of Bunter.

His glance went to the cake that Bunter was devouring, with an expression which showed that he was hungry.

Bunter gave a sniff.

"Who the thump are you?" he demanded.

The boy stared at him without answering. He seemed alarmed at having come on anyone in that secluded and solitary spot.

"Can't you speak?" sneered Bunter.

The boy nodded.

"Well, speak, then, you scarecrow! Who are you?"

"Ragged Dick."

"Great pip! Is that your name?" ejaculated Bunter.

The young vagrant nodded again.

"What a name!" said Bunter. "Well, Ragged Dick – he, he, he! – take yourself off! You don't look quite clean enough for a fellow to want your company. Don't you know you're trespassing here?"

This was rather cool of Bunter, as he was a trespasser himself. But he could see that the ragged youth did not know that.

"I—I suppose so," muttered Ragged Dick. "I—I dodged into the park to get away from somebody, sir."

Bunter raised a fat forefinger.

"A bobby, I suppose?" he said. "You've been stealing!"

Ragged Dick flushed crimson.

"I haven't! I—I've been beaten because I wouldn't steal chickens. That's why I've cleared off."

"Gammon!" said Bunter.

Ragged Dick backed away, but the cake seemed to draw him, and he stepped in again.

"Hungry?" asked Bunter. The Owl of the Remove was not much given to considering others, but even Bunter could feel for a fellow who was hungry. It was such an awful thing, as he knew by experience of occasions when he had had nothing between dinner and tea.

Dick nodded.

"You keep your distance," said Bunter warningly. "You look quite capable of stealing this cake."

This again was rather cool of Bunter, considering how the cake had come into his possession.

"I wouldn't steal a crumb," said Dick. "But I'm hungry. I haven't eaten since yesterday morning."

"My hat!"

Bunter was really touched.

He broke off a chunk of cake and held it out to the ragged youth.

"There you are!" he said.

Ragged Dick hesitated to take it, hungry as he was. But his grimy fingers finally closed on it.

"Take it!" snapped Bunter. "I don't mind giving you charity if you're only a beggar and not a pickpocket."

Bunter meant this delicate speech to be kind. His kindness seemed rather unappreciated by its recipient, however. Ragged Dick's eyes gleamed at him.

"I'm not a beggar!" he exclaimed.

"Oh, rats!" sneered Bunter. "What else are you, I'd like to know? Trespassing here and nosing after a fellow's grub."

"I'm hungry," said Ragged Dick. "But I wouldn't take anything as a beggar. I'd almost as soon steal. You can take your cake back, sir."

"Likely to, after your dirty fingers have touched it," said Bunter disdainfully. "Take it and clear off, you cheeky young cad!"

Whiz!

"Yarooh!" roared Bunter.

The chunk of cake came whizzing at Bunter, and it landed fairly on his fat little nose.

"There's your cake!" said Ragged Dick. "Take it, and keep a civil tongue in your head."

"Yow-ow!" gasped Bunter.

He rubbed his fat little nose furiously and jumped up. Bunter was not exactly a fighting-man, but his nose was not to be assaulted by a ragged fellow who looked as if he had

32

picked himself up from a scrap-heap. The Owl of the Remove clenched his fat fists and advanced on the vagrant.

"You cheeky rotter – "

"Oh, cheese it!" said Ragged Dick.

"I'll jolly well – "

The vagrant backed away.

"Better keep off," he said. "I don't want to hurt you. But – "

But a retreat was all that Bunter needed to encourage him to the point of heroism. He rushed at the ragged youth, hitting out.

Crash!

Bunter's blow was knocked up, and a hard fist was planted on his chest, knocking him back into the summer-house. He sat down there, with a heavy bump.

"Ow!" gasped Bunter.

Ragged Dick grinned at him.

"I told you it would be better to keep off!" he said. "Ow! Wow!"

"Keep a civil tongue in your head when you're talking to a bloke down on his luck!" said Dick.

"I–I–I'll have you run in!" gasped Bunter. "You're a trespasser, and a pickpocket, and a ruffian! Ow! Beast! You come back, and I'll jolly well give you a licking!"

But Ragged Dick was gone.

Billy Bunter picked himself up, gasping for breath. He sat down on the old bench again, and it was some little time before he resumed munching the cake. His fat face glowed with indignation. He, William George Bunter, a Greyfriars fellow, had actually been punched – actually knocked down – by a ragged scarecrow – a tramp thick with the dirt and dust of the country lanes. Really, it was almost time for the skies to fall!

But the Owl of the Remove recovered his equanimity at last, and gave his attention to the cake once more.

It disappeared at last.

The last crumb and the last plum vanished, and Bunter leaned back in his seat, to rest after his exertions. His eyes closed behind his glasses, and he began to snore.

He dreamed pleasantly of unlimited feeds at the school shop. But from his pleasant dreams he had a rude awakening.

He came out of the land of dreams with a sudden shake, and started up, with a vague impression that the ragged youth had returned.

"Leggo, you beast!" he howled. "I'll jolly well lick you! I'll have your run in, you scoundrel!"

"What—what!"

"Oh, crumbs!" gasped Bunter.

A tall gentleman in shooting clothes stood before him, with a cigarette in his mouth. The dark, angry, wrinkled face stared down at Bunter; a sinewy hand was shaking him by a fat shoulder. With a quake of terror Bunter realised that this was Sir Henry Compton, and that the crusty old gentleman had caught him trespassing.

"What? What? What are you doing here?" snorted the old gentleman, shaking Bunter.

"I—I—I'm not here – "

"What?"

"I—I mean – Leggo! Ow!"

"You are a trespasser, sir!" thundered Sir Henry.

"I—I—I– "

Shake! Shake!

"Leave my grounds at once! If you are not outside my park gates in five minutes, I will give you in charge, by gad!"

"Oh!" gasped Bunter. "I—I—I'm going!"

"Go!"

The Owl of the Remove fairly jumped out of the summer-house. He ran into the arms of a man in gaiters, who caught him by the collar.

"Jenks!"

"Yes, Sir Henry!"

"See that trespassing young rascal off the estate! Then go up to the house and wait for a telegram. If it comes, bring it to me at once."

"Yes, Sir Henry!"

The baronet sat down on the bench vacated by Bunter and lighted a fresh cigarette. William George Bunter, with Jenks' heavy hand on his collar, was marched away. Jenks opened a gate in the park wall, and, without a word, but with a hefty drive of his boot, helped Bunter into the road.

Bunter sat down there and roared.

The gate closed on him.

"Ow!" gasped the hapless Owl of the Remove.

He picked himself up dismally, and started on a five-mile tramp back to Greyfriars. Long before a mile had elapsed under his lagging feet, William George Bunter felt that his happy picnic in Compton Park had been hardly earned.

CHAPTER 5

A Strange Meeting!

RAGGED DICK stirred in a bed of bracken and shook himself and rose.

The sun was down. In the east, silvery moonlight stole over the sky. Night dews were falling in Compton Park; the youthful vagrant shivered as he picked himself up.

Round him were great trees and deep shadows. In the gloom of the thickly-wooded park many fellows might have been perplexed to find their way. But Ragged Dick was at no loss. For as long as he could remember he had had no home; the fields and woods and lanes had been his home in the summer days; streets and railway-arches in the winter-time. He moved away through the gloomy wood unerringly.

He was heading for the solitary summer-house where he had encountered Bunter. By that time, he was assured, the fellow would have gone, and it was unlikely that the lonely little shelter would have another visitor after dark. Slight shelter as it was, it was better than the open park, with the dew falling, and Ragged Dick intended to pass the night there, stretched on the bench. He had no better refuge, and he was reluctant to venture upon the open roads again, for fear of falling in with Pedlar Parker. He was hungry, but often and often the outcast had been hungry before; it was no new hardship for him.

With silent footsteps, almost like some slinking animal of the night, Ragged Dick drew nearer to the little shelter under the oaks and beeches. As he drew close to it, a faint scent came to his keen nostrils. The scent of tobacco. He halted.

Dark as it was, someone was in the summer-house, smoking. As he peered through the tangled creepers, he could see a tiny red glow – the tip of a cigarette. The waif stood, hesitating.

It was not Bunter who was here – he was sure of that. He had seen that Bunter was a schoolboy, and a schoolboy was not likely to linger in the lonely old park after nightfall. But someone was there, and it was no refuge for the outcast, after all.

But he was tired – tired and hungry, and in a mood of deep gloom. Used as he was to wandering at all hours of day and night, he was weary of wandering now. He did not move back – he leaned on the thick trunk of an oak, only a few yards from the man, unseen, sitting on the bench in the summer-house – unseen save for the glowing tip of the cigarette.

He hardly cared if the man found him there – if the man were a keeper or the master of the estate. He was too gloomy and reckless to care. But the man did not move. The scent of tobacco came through the leaves and twigs as the cigarette was smoked away, and the red tip died to a mere spark, and then into blackness.

He heard the unseen man stir then, and quivered back a little farther into the thick greenery around him. If the man was leaving, his refuge would be open to him; he did not want to be seen. But the man did not step out.

Ragged Dick heard a sound from him – a deep, prolonged sigh, that seemed to come from a troubled laboured heart.

He started slightly at the sound. He wondered who it was, hidden in the darkness of the interior, whose heart was so heavy.

A match flared.

Through the interstices of the thick creepers Dick could see into the summer-house, now that there was a light.

The man was lighting a fresh cigarette.

Dick saw him in the light of the match — a tall, somewhat gaunt man, of advanced age, with a grim, imperious face and heavy brows — a man handsome, in spite of his many years. well dressed in shooting clothes; a man who looked wealthy and masterful. The face was brown and wrinkled. The hand that held the cigarette was well kept, but gnarled with age. It trembled slightly.

The match went out.

Again there was a red glow of the cigarette-end, the only spot of light in the dense gloom.

Dick stood silent against the oak.

This was no keeper. Evidently it was the master of the great estate upon which the waif had trespassed. A man who had been in great authority all his long life, from his looks, and had never brooked dispute or contradiction; a man whose own iron will was his law; a man who was little likely to show mercy or ruth to a homeless waif trespassing in his park — little likely to sympathise with, or even to understand, the feelings of men less fortunately placed in the world. And yet this man, evidently wealthy, lord of a great domain, was heavy of heart. Life was bitter to him, too, as that heavy sigh had shown. In his different sphere, probably his troubles were as great as those of the homeless waif — perhaps greater.

The waif remained where he was, silent; while, in the summer-house, the master of Compton Hall smoked one cigarette after another — a reckless self-indulgence which probably accounted for the trembling of his hands, for in other respects his years did not seem to have told on him.

Suddenly there was a footstep and a brushing of twigs. Someone was coming to the summer-house.

Dick shrunk a little deeper into the dark greenery.

A voice, deep and resonant, was heard:

"Is that you, Jenks?"

"Yes, Sir Henry."

"Is there a telegram?"

"I have brought it, Sir Henry?"

A shadow passed into the summer-house.

"Give me a light."

An electric torch gleamed out in the gloom of the little interior. Through the screen of twigs and leaves Dick saw the brown old hand take the telegram. A half-smoked cigarette was flung on the ground.

But the old baronet was in no hurry to open the envelope.

"Leave the torch here, Jenks. You may go."

"Yes, Sir Henry."

The keeper went the way he had come.

There was deep silence as his footsteps died away in the distance.

The little beam of electric light glowed in the gloom. It was several minutes before Ragged Dick heard the sound of an envelope torn open. Then the old man's voice came to his ears.

"Dead!"

The waif's heart throbbed.

The beam of the electric torch, lying on the seat, fell partly on the bowed figure of Sir Henry Compton.

The telegram fluttered to the ground.

"Dead!"

Then, after a long pause:

"Poor boy!"

Ragged Dick – ragged, homeless, hungry – felt a throb of compassion for the wealthy baronet, the master of Compton Hall. It was some terrible news that had been brought by the telegram.

The waif moved silently away.

He was no longer thinking of the summer-house as a shelter for the night. Waif and tramp and vagrant as he was, Ragged Dick had a delicacy of feeling that would not allow him to intrude on a stricken man's grief.

But as he moved away in the darkness there came a strange sound behind him – a strange, gurgling, choking sound. He halted.

There was a fall.

In an instant Dick was springing back. The old man had fallen to the ground, and choking sounds came from his throat. The blow he had received had been too much for him.

Dick was kneeling beside him in a moment, the electric torch in his hand. He was startled and scared, but his only thought was to help the man in the grip of a sudden seizure.

The old baronet was writhing on the ground, his hands clutching and grappling as if at an unseen enemy; his face crimson and suffocated. His eyes were still intelligent, however, and they gleamed at the boy bending over him. He could not speak, but he made a struggling gesture towards his throat, and Dick understood. He tore at the old man's collar, and freed his throat, and then lifted his head and rested it on his ragged knee.

It was all that he could do. There was no help at hand. A terrible fear was in his heart that the old man might die there as he lay – that he was only easing the last moments of an old man in the grip of the King of Terrors.

But the struggling breath of the baronet grew more even and calm. Minutes that seemed like hours crawled by, and then the old man spoke in faint, gasping tones:

"There is a flask in my coat. Get it."

"Yes, sir!" breathed Dick.

He groped in the pockets and found the flask.

"Open it."

Dick unscrewed the stopper.

"Give it to me."

Sir Henry Compton sipped from the flask, and then, at a gesture from the old man, Dick drew it away.

He waited, still supporting the heavy head on his knee. The baronet was recovering now.

"Help me to the bench," he said at last.

Dick helped him up silently. The master of Compton Hall was a heavy weight, but the waif was strong and sturdy. Sir Henry was seated on the bench at last.

He sat there, leaning back, breathing hard and deep.

Dick hesitated.

"Shall I go for help, sir?"

"No."

"But you need — "

"I know best what I need."

Dick was silent. The old man was recovering; his masterful will was as strong as ever. Sir Henry Compton was almost himself again now.

"Do you want me any more, sir?" asked Dick at last timidly.

"No."

Dick backed out of the summer-house. But the deep voice of the old baronet followed him.

"Stop!"

Dick turned back.

"Who are you?" asked Sir Henry Compton, peering at him in the gloom from under his grey, wrinkled brows. "You have helped me when I needed it. But who are you, and how did you come here?"

"I am a tramp."

"You are young for tramping the roads," said Sir Henry. "Have you no home?"

"No."

"Your name?"

"Dick."

"What else?" snapped the old man impatiently.

41

"Nothing else," said the waif quietly. "I've been called Ragged Dick. That's all."

"Have you no parents?"

"No."

"Or relations?"

"No."

"How do you live?"

"Tramping, picking up jobs – all sorts of things."

"Begging and stealing among them, I have no doubt."

"No," said Dick quietly.

He waited, but as the old man did not speak again, he made a move to go. But the deep voice called him back.

"Stay, I tell you."

Ragged Dick stayed.

"You have given me aid when I needed it," said Sir Henry. "You look as if you need aid yourself. I shall see that you are cared for before you leave my land."

"I am not a beggar, sir," said Dick quietly. "If you could give me any work to do on your land, I should be grateful. But I have never taken anything in charity, and I never will. You had better let me go, sir."

"The times are changed," said the old man sardonically. "Even the vagrants of the roads are insolent to their betters."

"I did not mean to be insolent, sir," said Dick, colouring. "But I have never been a beggar."

"And you are homeless, ragged, tattered, doubtless hungry!" The old man seemed to be speaking to himself. "Yet you live – and my grandson, with all that wealth could provide for him, has died. He is dead – and this starving vagrant lives!" He broke into a bitter laugh. "Dead – and the Compton lands must pass to an idle, dissolute waster, a shame and disgrace to his name – and this homeless wretch lives to haunt the roads and starve and steal!"

There was a long silence after the muttered words, and Ragged Dick stood uneasily, longing to go, yet held by the authority of the old man's command. Sir Henry rose at last from the bench. The torch flickered out. A match was struck, and Sir Henry lighted a cigarette.

"May I go now, sir?" muttered Dick.

"No!" The voice was hard and grim. "You have assisted me, and I do not choose to be under an obligation. It shall be for your benefit that you trespassed on my land."

"But – "

"Silence! Come with me!"

There was command in the old autocrat's voice that was not to be gain-said. He strode away, a tall, grim figure in the gloom, and the little waif obediently followed him.

CHAPTER 6

The Good Samaritan!

" I SAY, you fellows – "
"Hallo, hallo, hallo! Here he is!"
"You fat villain – "
"Collar him!"

Billy Bunter jumped back.

He met the Famous Five as they came up the Remove passage, and he met them with his most ingratiating and propitiatory smile. But the chums of the Remove did not seem to be in a mood to be propitiated.

"I–I say, you fellows, hold on!" exclaimed Bunter.

"That's what we're going to do!" grinned Bob Cherry.

And he held on to Bunter's collar.

"Bring him into the study," said Harry Wharton.

"Yarooh! I say, Toddy, rescue!" roared Bunter, as he was propelled towards the doorway of Study No. 1.

Peter Todd, looking out of Study No. 7, grinned.

"What's the row?" he asked.

"The fat bounder burgled our picnic!" growled Johnny Bull.

"Ha, ha, ha!"

"It's not a laughing matter," roared Johnny Bull indignantly. "We're famished."

"The famishfulness is terrific!"

"It's a misunderstanding!" gasped Bunter. "I—I never bagged the tuck, you know. I wouldn't! You see – "

"Roll him in. I've got a fives bat for him," said Wharton.

"Yarooh! Help an old pal, Peter – "

Peter Todd chuckled.

"Keep your fat paws from picking and stealing, old fat man," he answered. "Don't I keep on giving you that advice?"

"Beast!"

Peter went back into his study, apparently not keen to distinguish himself in the role of rescuer. Vernon-Smith and Tom Redwing came up the stairs together, and stopped to look on as Bunter was propelled into Study No. 1.

"Smithy, old chap, lend a fellow a hand!" yelled Bunter.

The Bounder grinned.

"Will a foot do?" he asked.

"Whooop!"

Smithy lent a foot, and Bunter rolled into the study and sprawled on the carpet.

Nugent closed the door.

Bunter sat up, with five wrathful faces looking down on him. The captain of the Remove picked up a fives bat.

"Shove him across a chair," he said.

"I say, Harry, old chap – "

"If you call me Harry, old chap, you fat worm, I'll give you one extra."

"Bob, old man – "

"Cheese it!"

"I—I say, you fellows – "

Four pairs of hands grasped the Owl of the Remove, and he was extended, wriggling, across a chair, in a favourable position for the application of a fives bat.

"Yow-ow-ow! Let a fellow speak!" howled Bunter. "Can't you let a chap explain, you beasts?"

"What is there to explain?" demanded Bob Cherry. "You bolted with our tuck, and we had to walk home all the way from Compton Park without our tea."

"While you were scoffing the grub, you fat cannibal!" exclaimed Johnny Bull ferociously.

"I—I say, I was awfully hungry when I got in, you know," gasped Bunter. "I don't believe I should have got in at all, only I got a lift in the carrier's cart. And I was too late for tea, and that beast Toddy wouldn't lend me a bob, and my postal-order hasn't come, and now — "

"And now you're going to have a dozen with this bat to complete the tale of woe!" chuckled Bob. "Lay it on!"

"Hold on!" yelled Bunter. "Let a fellow explain. I—I didn't scoff the tuck, you know — I wouldn't!"

"Where is it, then?" demanded Wharton.

"I—I say, you fellows, I—I— Let a fellow speak! I—I can explain the whole thing," gasped Bunter.

"Rot!"

"Bosh!"

"Give him a dozen, and let him explain afterwards," said Johnny Bull. "It will only be gammon, anyhow."

"Honest Injun!" yelled Bunter. "Look here, this isn't the way to treat a chap who's been helping the poor, and feeding the hungry, and all that!"

"What!"

In their astonishment, the juniors released Bunter. He squirmed off the chair and set his big spectacles straight on his fat little nose and blinked at them indignantly.

Owing to the windfall of a lift in the carrier's cart, Bunter had reached Greyfriars well ahead of the Famous Five, and he had had time to think out his defence. Bunter and the truth had never been well acquainted, and the greater the scrape in which the Owl found himself, the farther and farther he departed from veracity.

But Bunter had the gift — very valuable to an habitual deceiver — of taking his own tremendous "whoppers" seriously. Having thought out what he considered to be a good yarn, he considered that fellows ought to believe it, and almost believed it himself by this time. So he was feeling quite genuinely indignant as he blinked at the five Removites.

"I say, you fellows, I expected you to take it a bit more decently," he said. "Of course, a fellow doesn't like to lose a spread. I shouldn't myself. But when a poor chap's starving, what's a really kind-hearted and generous fellow to do?"

"Eh?"

"What?"

"Do you want us to believe that you gave that feed away?" asked Bob Cherry, almost dazedly.

"Exactly!"

"Oh, my hat!"

"Great pip! That's the limit, even for Bunter!" exclaimed Harry Wharton, staring at the Owl of the Remove. "You don't really expect us to get that down, Bunter?"

"I suppose you can take my word!" said Bunter, with dignity.

"Your word! Oh, crumbs!"

"Oh, really, Wharton — "

"Let's hear the yarn," said Bob, with a chuckle. "We'll give him six extra for telling lies if he doesn't prove his case. Now, then, go ahead, Bunter!"

"I say, you fellows — "

"Cut it short!" growled Johnny Bull.

"You—you see — " gasped Bunter.

"We don't see," said Nugent. "We are waiting to see."

"If you'd seen that ragged kid, you'd have been sorry for him," said Bunter impressively. "A poor kid, you know — chap about our own age — homeless and hungry and starving and famished, and—and in want of food."

"Must have been in want of food if he was hungry as well as starving and famished," agreed Bob Cherry. "Get on with it, without piling on the agony too thick."

"Oh, really, Cherry — "

"Buck up!" roared Johnny Bull. "We've got to wallop you before tea, and I want my tea!"

"Oh, really, Bull – "

"Give him the bat – "

"I say, I'm explaining as fast as I can, ain't I?" yelled Bunter. "I tell you you'd have felt sorry for that chap."

"What chap?"

"Ragged Dick!" said Bunter.

"What?"

"That's what he called himself – a poor tramp, you know, homeless and nameless and hungry and – "

"Have you come across that kid Ragged Dick?" asked Harry Wharton, in astonishment.

For once Bunter found believers. The Famous Five knew that Ragged Dick had a real existence, and was not a mere figment of Bunter's fertile imagination. Bunter's task was easier than he had anticipated, as he had known nothing of the affair with Ragged Dick and Pedlar Parker. He had not even taken the trouble to wonder what had called the juniors away when they had so fortunately left him alone with the tuck. All he knew was that some person unknown had been yelling in a field, and that they had run to the scene.

"That's what he called himself," said Bunter – "Ragged Dick. What a name, you know! Ragged and hungry and starving and famished – "

"We've had that before!" grunted Johnny Bull. "Look here, we'd have handed over that feed to that poor kid without waiting to be asked if we'd had the chance. If you did – "

"Just what I did," said Bunter. "I–I was going to take a snack, and then he came up, and–and I – you know my generous nature – "

"Phew!"

"I gave him the lot," said Bunter. "I said: 'Here you are, kid!' and handed it over to him. He thanked me with tears rolling down his cheeks."

"Rats!" – from Johnny Bull.

"If you don't believe me, Bull, you can ask the fellow himself."

"Where is he, then?"

"How should I know?"

"You silly ass! How can I ask him when I shan't ever see him again?" demanded Johnny Bull.

"Look here! If this is true, all serene!" said Harry Wharton. "We're jolly hungry, but we wouldn't mind handing over our feed to a chap who was hungrier. But you're not built that way, Bunter, and it's too jolly steep."

"Oh, really, Wharton – "

"Good Samaritan – I don't think!" grunted Johnny Bull. "Looks like it, doesn't he? Good Samaritans don't grow as fat as Bunter!"

"Ha, ha, ha!"

"Now, as it happens, we saw that kid Ragged Dick," went on Wharton. "We collared a pedlar chap who was whacking him, and gave him a chance to get away."

"Oh!" ejaculated Bunter.

"He cleared off before we could get a look at him," said Harry. "You had cleared off with the grub, too – "

"I–I– "

"You'd cleared off when I looked for you," said Bob. "And that ragged kid was out of sight, too. Where did you meet him, if you met him at all?"

"In Compton Park," said Bunter.

"You trespassed in the park?"

"I–I told you Sir Henry was an old friend of my pater's," said Bunter. "I just dropped in – "

"Oh, can it!" growled Johnny Bull.

"It's likely enough that the kid dodged over the palings into the park to get clear," said Harry, "and that's where Bunter went, of course, to get away with the grub. So you came on Ragged Dick in the park. I dare say that much is true, as you were both there at the same time. But you didn't hand him the feed, you fat fabricator!"

"If you'd seen him — "

"We did see him, ass, before he cleared off."

"Well, then, you ought to be able to understand how I–I pitied him," said Bunter. "It–it would have done you good to see him eat! It would, really! Fairly bolted it, you know, and I–I stood by, you know, helping him and not touching a morsel myself. I thought that you fellows wouldn't really mind letting the grub go to feed the hungry — "

"We wouldn't," said Frank Nugent.

"So it's all right, then," said Bunter brightly. "You say yourselves you'd have given him the grub. So what have you got to complain about?"

The Famous Five eyed Bunter.

But for the fact that they had met Ragged Dick themselves, certainly they would not have believed a word of the story from beginning to end. But there was, at least, a nucleus of truth in Bunter's yarn. It was clear that he had met the waif– whether he had played the Good Samaritan or not.

"After all, if he whacked the grub out with that hungry kid, that's something for Bunter!" said Bob Cherry.

"Yes. But — "

"You should have seen him eat!" said Bunter impressively. "It would really have done you good!"

"Pity we didn't see it!" agreed Johnny Bull. "We might have believed you then."

"Oh, really, Bull — "

"Shall we give the fat villain the benefit of the doubt?" asked Bob Cherry, looking round at his comrades.

"I don't think you ought to doubt my word, Cherry. As for the grub, of course, I shall pay for it when my postal-order comes. I'm expecting it by the first post to-morrow morning. And I tell you what — I'll use my influence with Sir Henry to get you fellows asked to Compton Hall, I will, really!"

"You silly Owl!"

"And I must say I'm a little shocked at you!

"What?"

"It seems to me that you grudge that feed to a hungry, starving, and famished chap," said Bunter severely. "I call that shocking!"

"Why, you cheeky fat villain — "

"As for the value of it, I'll settle that out of my postal-order. I certainly do not want you mean fellows to pay for my—my charitable actions!" said Bunter loftily. "Mean — that's what you are! One of the eggs was whiffy, too! I shan't pay for that one; I couldn't eat it."

"You couldn't eat it?" said Bob, staring at him.

"No, I couldn't!"

"But the others were all right, were they?"

"Well, I've tasted better," said Bunter. "As a matter of fact, it wasn't much of a feed, though you fellows make such a song about it. The cake was gritty."

"Was it?"

"Yes, it was. And the lemonade was thin stuff, and didn't have enough sugar in it. Muck, in fact!"

"Have you ever heard the proverb that liars should have good memories, Bunter?" inquired Bob.

"Eh?"

"Did Ragged Dick tell you that the egg was whiffy, and that the cake was gritty, and that there wasn't enough sugar in the lemonade?"

"While he was thanking you with tears rolling down his cheeks?" roared Johnny Bull.

"Eh! I—I mean — "

"Up-end him!"

"Yarooooh!"

Bunter went across the chair again. As usually happened with the hapless Ananias of Greyfriars, he had given himself away after an elaborate series of inventions. The chums of the Remove had been prepared to give him the benefit of the doubt. But there was no longer any doubt; so they gave him the benefit of the fives-bat.

Whack, whack, whack!

"Woop! I say, you fellows – "

Whack!

"Yaroooh! I say, I really did give him some cake and it wasn't my fault he chucked it at me – "

Whack!

"Yow-ow-ow! You beast, stoppit! I've been kicked – you-ow! – in the same place – yow-ow-ow! That beast of a keeper, you know!"

Whack!

"Yarooooooooo!"

"Does Sir Henry Compton let his keepers kick his distinguished guests?" chuckled Johnny Bull.

"Ha, ha, ha!"

"Yow-ow-ow-ow-woooooopp!"

Bunter rolled off the chair. He backed into the doorway, and shook a fat fist at the Famous Five.

"Ow! Beasts! I won't pay for the grub now, when my postal-order comes! I was going to, and now I won't! Beasts!"

And Billy Bunter rolled wrathfully away, after delivering that Parthian shot, leaving the chums of the Remove chuckling, and not at all dismayed by the prospect of losing their just share in Bunter's celebrated postal-order – when it came!

CHAPTER 7

The Spendthrift!

"MR. ROGER COMPTON!"

Sir Henry turned his wrinkled face, with something like a snarl upon it, towards the gentleman who was shown into the library at Compton Hall.

He did not rise from the deep-backed chair in which he sat by the crackling log fire. There was no welcome in his looks – no courtesy in his manner.

He fixed his eyes on the man who came towards him, with a glint of animosity in them, under his grizzled, wrinkled brows.

The visitor was a man of perhaps forty, though at the first glance he looked younger. He was dressed well, almost fastidiously – a contrast to the baronet, who, late as the hour was in the evening, had not changed out of his shooting-clothes. The man had been handsome, but there were very visible signs in his face of a loose and reckless life. He came towards the grim old baronet, and held out a well-manicured hand, which Sir Henry Compton did not touch.

"Come, come, cousin Henry!" said Mr. Roger Compton. "You will not shake hands with your kinsman?"

"Kinsman or no, I will not touch your hand!" said Sir Henry. "It was in my mind to refuse even to open my door to you, Roger Compton. Why are you here?"

53

Roger Compton smiled — a smile that was not pleasant.

"How long is it since we have met?" he answered. "Finding myself at Courtfield — "

"For the races?" interposed Sir Henry, with a curl of the lip.

"Precisely — for the races, precisely! Finding myself there, as I said, I decided to see my nearest relative before I left, and to ask — "

"To ask — what?"

"After your grandson, Sir Henry — little Richard, whose delicate health has caused me more concern than you may have supposed."

The baronet's face set hard.

"I quite understand your interest in my grandson's health," he assented — "quite!" His hands pressed his breast for a moment, where, in an inner pocket, reposed a crumpled telegram — the telegram that had announced the death of his grandson. "A delicate boy's life is all that stands between you and Compton Hall — when once an obstinate old man is laid with his fathers."

Roger Compton made a deprecating gesture.

"I should scarcely look on the matter in that light, Sir Henry," he murmured.

"You would scarcely look on it in any other," retorted the baronet. "I know you, Roger! I have known you from your youth upwards, and never known any good of you. Is there a disreputable night club in London, a race-course in the country, where you are not known for what you are — gambler, blackguard, adventurer, a disgrace to the name you bear!"

"As bitter as ever, Sir Henry!" said Roger.

He sank into a chair; the grim, old master of Compton Hall had not even asked him to be seated.

"Quite! Again I ask, why are you here? Have you any reason to suppose that my grandson is worse, and that you are nearer to your inheritance?" said Sir Henry sardonically.

And again his hand crushed the crumpled telegram which had shattered all his hopes of keeping the Compton estate out of the hands of the man he despised and detested.

"I know that Richard is delicate – that his life for years has been spent with doctors and nurses," said Roger. "I am naturally anxious to know whether he shows signs of being restored to health. And – little as you may believe me – I feel for your deep anxiety concerning him!"

There was a sneer with the last words.

"I have had time to become used to my anxiety," said the old man composedly. "I have seen little of my grandson – and I am not of an affectionate nature, as you know. You know, too, that I should think little of him, if it were not that he alone stood between you and Compton Hall when I am gone."

"I am aware that you would disinherit me, if the entail were not too strict!" sneered Roger.

"And I am aware," said the old man, "that you, the last of the line, will have power to break the entail, and break up the property that has been in our family since the time of Edward the First. I am aware that your countless creditors would drive you to do so, even if you had not decency to respect your name – which you have not. I am aware that but for my grandson, when I go, everything goes, and the Comptons will disappear for ever. I am aware of all that, Roger – a stranger will rule here when I am gone, while you waste the proceeds of your baseness in drink and gaming. If there were any means – "

He broke off, biting his lip.

Roger Compton smiled again.

"If there were any means to get rid of your cousin and heir, you would not hesitate," he said.

"No."

"Fortunately for me, there are no means," smiled Roger.

"If Richards dies — "

"If!" muttered Sir Henry.

"And I have a right to know how he stands," said Roger. "I learn that for the past year he has been in a foreign country — in the hands of medical specialists. I am entitled to know more. He is now of age to be placed at school — more than of an age for that. It may be taken as a matter of course that he will be sent to Greyfriars, as his father was before him. Is he going to Greyfriars?"

"That is my business!"

"Mine, too, if you will excuse me, Sir Henry!"

"What rights have you over my grandson?" demanded the old baronet, with a fierce bending of the brows.

"None! But I have a right to know how the matter stands, and" — Roger Compton paused a moment — "where he is, and whether he still lives. I do not know that for a fact; you have told me nothing. If my young cousin Richard no longer lives — "

"The moneylenders would grant you better terms in that case," said Sir Henry sardonically.

"Exactly. For that reason, if for no other, I require to know more of the boy Richard," said Roger coolly.

Sir Henry Compton rose to his feet.

"You will know nothing from me," he said. "We have never been friends, Roger, and now we are enemies. If you come here again I shall give orders that you are not to be admitted."

"You will tell me nothing of Richard?"

"Nothing!"

The spendthrift's eyes gleamed.

"I shall make inquiries, then — "

"Make them!"

"You lead me to suspect — "

"Suspect what you please. But go!" said Sir Henry grimly. "After my death you may disgrace Compton Hall with your

56

presence; while I live I am master here!" He touched a bell. "Walton, show this gentleman out. And if he should call again I am not at home."

Roger Compton rose, his eyes glittering, his cheeks pale with rage and mortification.

Without a word he walked out of the library.

The door closed.

Sir Henry sank back into the deep chair. His brows were knitted, black, and gloomy.

He had refused to give the heir of Compton Hall the information he sought. But he must learn it ere long; the announcement of Richard Compton's death would enlighten him. He would know that only an old man stood between him and the estate; his creditors would know, his moneylenders would know. It would mean a fresh accession of borrowed wealth for the spendthrift — a fresh orgy of waste and reckless extravagance, to be paid for when the Compton estate came into his hands, when the entail could be broken, and the lands sold, the ancient house given to a stranger. Some newly-rich profiteer would dwell where generations of Comptons had lived and died — while the last of the race was drinking himself to death.

Was there no way out?

If the boy had lived — and he had lived only to nearly fifteen years, and then all that medical skill could do, all that a soft Southern climate could do to save him, had failed.

The hard old man had seen little of the hapless boy, had cared little for him; cared only for him as a Compton, to carry on the name and save the estate. All that there was of softness or affection in his nature was buried with his only son.

To save the old estate from the clutches of Roger Compton and a ravenous crew of usurers — that was almost an obsession in the old man's mind now. Had he been able to will it away he would have willed it to the veriest stranger rather than to the dissolute blackguard who was his natural heir.

But he had not the power. Comptons dead and gone long ago had tied up the estate too carefully, to keep the lands in the family, to preserve the family name, never foreseeing or dreaming that a Compton might be the one to bring ruin and oblivion upon the old name.

Was there no way out?

Long the old man sat there, thinking, thinking, with wrinkled brows, his hands clenched on the dark oak arms of the chair. Was there no way? No way to keep up the old house, to keep the wide estate together, to save it from the gambler and his hungry crew? If his grandson had lived, if he had had another grandson, if he had had the power to make an heir of an adopted son; if he had been able, by any stratagem or trickery, to cheat the law laid down by dead men long ago, by a secret adoption – But Roger Compton was not the man to be deceived. And yet –

In the dark recesses of the old man's troubled brain the scheme was born at last. His grandson had died in a foreign land. No one in England knew of the death – could know until he chose to tell. What if he did not tell? What if the lad appeared at Compton Hall in the name of Richard Compton; went to Greyfriars School as Richard Compton – Richard restored to health – Richard, grandson of Sir Henry and heir of Compton Hall?

His eyes glittered fiercely under his knitted, grey brows.

Better that than the breaking-up of the old estate to satisfy a hungry crew of moneylenders, to provide Roger with a last wild orgy to wind up his career of riotous black-guardism.

But how?

And then into the baronet's mind came the remembrance of a boy's face that had bent over him in his seizure in the old summer-house in the park – the boy whom he had placed for lodgings in his keeper's house.

A boy unknown, nameless, friendless, forlorn; all that he

needed for his purpose!

Long into the night the baronet sat, staring into the dying fire.

When he rose at last his plan was formed and fixed, irrevocable – the plan that was to save Compton Hall from the spendthrift, and to bring about an amazing change in the fortunes of Ragged Dick.

CHAPTER 8

A Dazzling Prospect!

"SEND the boy in!"

"Yes, Sir Henry!"

Jenks retired respectfully from his little parlour, into the window of which the morning sunlight gleamed.

Sir Henry Compton sat down.

He had given his instructions that the tattered lad was to be well cared for, and on the Compton estate Sir Henry's instructions were always carried out to the very letter.

Probably Jenks had been surprised by the baronet's concern for this wretched, ragged lad, whom he had brought to the lodge the evening before. It was not like Sir Henry Compton to trouble his lofty head about the poor and needy and friendless; it was more like him to drive them off his land without pity or ruth. Of the baronet's seizure, and of the aid the boy had given him, Jenks knew nothing. He did not know that the old man, hard as he was, did not choose to remain under an obligation; that his pride impelled him to pay richly for a service rendered. So far as Jenks was concerned, he only knew that it was Sir Henry's lordly will and pleasure that the homeless boy should be cared for – and cared for Ragged Dick had been under the keeper's roof.

He entered the little room a few minutes later rather timidly.

Sir Henry looked at him.

There was a change in the boy — a change so startling that he was scarcely recognisable. He was washed clean, his hair had been trimmed and combed, and he was dressed in a suit of clothes, plain but neat and good, that had belonged to the keeper's own boy, and had been given over to the waif.

Clean and neat clothes and boots in the place of his tattered rags made a wonderful difference; but still greater was the difference made by scrubbing and rubbing off the dirt and dust of the roads, trimming and combing the unkempt hair; still greater the difference brought about by plentiful food and a quiet and peaceful night's rest in a comfortable bed.

The baronet looked at the lad who stood before him as if scarcely able to believe his eyes.

Ragged Dick — no longer ragged — looked a handsome lad, well-set-up, sturdy, active, his face good-looking and pleasant in its expression, a little sunburnt, but so clean that it was clear that cleanliness was the boy's own taste, his previous griminess forced upon him by his wretched circumstances.

A smile of satisfaction came over the old man's face.

He had resolved upon his scheme — a scheme in which Ragged Dick was to play his part as an unconscious tool in his hands — a pawn in a game he did not understand. But doubts had troubled him. It was not easy, he realised, to change a slinking tramp into a fellow who could pass as a Compton, brought up in the lap of luxury. But he was re-assured upon that point now. This boy was no slinking tramp; circumstances had been against him, but he had the power of rising above his circumstances. The pride he had shown in his talk with the baronet the previous evening had offended the stiff old gentleman at the time; now it pleased him to remember it.

Pride that was, in his estimation, out of place in a ragged vagrant was an asset when that vagrant was to play the part of heir of Compton Hall.

For a good five minutes the baronet scanned the lad before him without speaking, but thinking deeply, more and more satisfied with the trend of his own thoughts.

Dick stood waiting uneasily.

The stern old brown face scared him a little; there was something awe-inspiring in this grim old man, though Dick was not easily scared.

What was wanted of him he could not guess.

So much kindness had been bestowed upon him, in return for the little service he had rendered for the old gentleman, that he was deeply grateful; and he had a hope that the old man was going to offer him employment on his estate.

A regular "job" on the land would have been enough to make the waif happy – he was not afraid of work, and he would have earned, and more than earned whatever the master of Compton Hall chose to pay him. To get off the roads, to keep himself clean and fit, to avoid such company as that of Pedlar Parker – the bare idea of it made Dick feel elated. To keep himself by his labour amid green woods and fields in the summer – Ragged Dick asked no more than that.

The baronet's long silence puzzled him

It did not need this long reflection for the old gentleman to make up his mind whether he was going to offer the vagrant a "job." Yet with what other intention could he have come to the keeper's lodge to see him?

Sir Henry spoke at last.

"Good–good, boy!" he said, apparently commenting on Dick's improved appearance. "Now, my boy, I have something to say to you – something very serious."

"Yes, sir," said Dick.

"You have told me that you have no relations, no parents, no name?"

Dick coloured a little.

"That is so, sir."

"Is there no one with a claim on you?"

"No, one, sir." The boy hesitated a moment. "For the last few weeks, sir, I've been tramping with a pedlar. But he had no claim on me."

"Where is he now?"

"I don't know, sir – gone, I hope. I ran away from him yesterday."

"Why?"

"He was a brute." Dick flushed. "He–he wanted me to steal chickens for him from the farm, and–and beat me because I wouldn't. Some schoolboys interfered, sir, and I got away from him and cleared off. That was why I came into your park, sir – to keep clear till the man was gone on his way."

Sir Henry gave him a searching look. "Is that the truth?"

Dick's lip quivered.

"If you don't believe me, sir, it's no use my saying anything," he answered. "It's the truth, but if you don't believe me, I suppose you won't give me a job. I can't give you any character."

"A–a what?" ejaculated Sir Henry. "Oh, you mean employment! I am not thinking of giving you employment."

Dick's face fell.

"Very well, sir," he said quietly. "I know I've no right to expect it. But after what you've done for me already I shall find it much easier to get work – looks mean a lot to a fellow like me, and I look respectable now. I hope you'll believe that I'm grateful, sir – and–and I'll go now."

"You will not go," said Sir Henry coldly. "Tell me once more – you are absolutely certain that no one who lives has a right to claim you?"

"I don't know of anyone, sir," answered Dick, surprised by the old man's inexplicable interest in such a detail.

"But you had a father once, I presume?"

"I suppose so, sir. I never knew him," said Dick.

"It's an odd story," said the baronet, eyeing him.

"There are plenty of fellows in the same boat, sir, if you look for them along the roads and hedges," said Dick.

"It is possible, I suppose. But you must have had some care in infancy. Have you had no education? Cannot you read or write? exclaimed Sir Henry, struck by a new difficulty.

Dick smiled.

"Oh, yes, sir! I've never been to school, but I've picked up a good deal — fellows can if they like. I once tramped on the road with a man who had been a Master of Arts at Oxford."

"A Master of Arts — tramping the roads!" exclaimed Sir Henry.

"There are all sorts on the roads, sir," said Dick. "A gentleman like you wouldn't know, sir. The man I'm speaking of was a drunkard — he had been to prison, too — he was a good man in his way, and I was with him for two or three years. He used to teach me when he was sober, and I used to take care of him when he was drunk."

"Good heavens!" muttered the old baronet. It was a glimpse of a life new and strange to the master of Compton Hall — as strange as the life of a different continent.

"He taught me a lot of things," said Dick. "You see, sir, I was keen to learn — I didn't want to be a tramp all my days. When he was drunk he used to spout Latin and Greek, and I asked him one day to teach me some Latin. He laughed and said he would — and he did, too. We hadn't any books, but I used to pick up old pieces of paper, and keep them for my exercises, and I learned Latin verses by heart from him — and he taught me some French, too. And I learned some more from a Frenchman I tramped with afterwards. I—I could do accounts, sir, if—if you wanted — "

"Where is he now?"

"I don't know, sir. He was run in."

"He was what?"

"I mean taken up by the police, sir, when he was drunk, and sent to chokey — I mean prison."

"What was his name?"

"Poynings, sir; but the tramps always called him Spouting Billy."

"How long since you have seen him?"

"More than a year, sir."

"He would scarcely know you again," said the baronet musingly. "Anyhow, a meeting would be very unlikely. Boy, what were you thinking of doing when you left here?"

"Looking for work, sir."

"What kind of work?"

"With the farmers, sir. A fellow can often pick up a job on the farms."

"Would you like to stay here?"

Dick's face brightened.

"I would, sir! If you would give me a job – I mean, employment, you'll find that I am honest, sir, and – "

"Tut, tut! Listen to me, my boy. See that that door is closed."

Dick looked to the door.

"Very good!" The baronet sank his voice a little. "I have reasons, my boy, which I do not choose to explain to you, for taking you under my care. You have no name – I shall give you my own name. You have no father – you will call me your grandfather. I shall adopt you as my grandson. But that will be a strict secret. All others will suppose that you are really my grandson, Richard Compton. Do you understand?"

Dick's eyes opened wide.

The baronet had asked him, did he understand, but assuredly he did not. His impression was that the old gentleman was wandering in his mind.

He stared blankly at the gnarled old face.

"Answer me, boy!" snapped Sir Henry. "You are not a fool, I hope. Do you understand what I say?"

"I–I – " stammered Dick helplessly.

"You are taken by surprise, of course!" said Sir Henry. "Listen to me carefully. I choose to adopt you as my grandson, and to make you, subject to good conduct, my heir—heir to these lands and to the house yonder. Heir to twenty thousand pounds a year if you please me, and if you prove yourself worthy of the position in which I think of placing you. You will go to a public school — Greyfriars School — you will go there as the grandson of Sir Henry Compton. Does that prospect please you?"

Dick almost tottered.

"You can't mean it, sir!" he panted.

"Do I look like a man who says what he does not mean?" almost snarled the old man.

"N-n-no, sir. But—but — "

"You are surprised — it is natural enough. You may take time to think it over, if you choose. But you will scarcely refuse such an offer, I presume?"

"Hardly, sir!" gasped Dick, in utter bewilderment. "But—but why should you do this for me, sir?"

"That is my own business, and you are not to ask questions. It is my will, and that is enough."

Ragged Dick gasped for breath. He was inclined to pinch himself to make sure that he was awake.

"But one caution, boy," said the baronet. "You are not to utter a word on this subject, or on the subject of your past. You are to be my grandson Richard — in name and in fact. That you are only my grandson by adoption is a secret. You understand?"

"Yes, sir," gasped Dick.

"I shall take you away from here immediately — to London. There you will be fitted out for school. I shall arrange with the headmaster of Greyfriars to admit you there as soon as practicable. By the time the holidays come round you will have shaken down into your new position. You will come here for the holidays as my grandson. You understand?"

Dick gasped.

"I will do anything you tell me, sir, of course. It seems like a dream to me what you are saying."

"No doubt – no doubt," said the baronet, more kindly. "But you will grow accustomed to it."

"But this keeper man, sir – Jenks, he knows – "

"Jenks will keep his own counsel," said Sir Henry. "You will say nothing to Jenks of what I have told you, and by the time you appear here as my grandson, Jenks will be gone."

Dick winced.

The old baronet, watching his face, read the thought that was passing in the boy's mind.

"So you have learned to think of others, tramping the roads," he said ironically. "But you need not trouble your head about Jenks. I am not the man to discharge a faithful servant to suit my own convenience. Jenks will be sent to my estate in Scotland, and he will not suffer."

"Yes, sir," gasped Dick.

"No one else here has seen you, and no one else will see you," said Sir Henry – "not till you come as if you were my grandson Richard, returning from school for the holidays." Sir Henry rose. "Not a word, mind. I rely upon your discretion. Make ready for a journey. In an hour I shall come to take you to London. Stay, I will not come for you here. Leave as if you were leaving for good, and wait for me at the railway-station."

"Yes, sir."

With a curt nod, the baronet left the room and the house.

Ragged Dick sank into a chair, his brain in a whirl.

Was it real, or was he dreaming? The adopted grandson of Sir Henry Compton. Heir to the lands upon which the previous day he had crept as a vagrant and a trespasser! It was a dream! It must be a dream!

The boy was still dazed when he left Compton Park and tramped to the railway-station. It was a dream. It must be a dream! But the tall, gaunt figure of Sir Henry Compton was there. He beckoned to Dick, and spoke a sharp word.

"Take your ticket to London. Here is the money. Join me at the London terminus."

That was all. And the baronet entered a first-class carriage. Ragged Dick travelled third, his brain still in a whirl.

It was not till the express disgorged its passengers at Charing Cross that he saw the baronet again. In the crowd on the platform Sir Henry beckoned to him, and they left the station together – Sir Henry to the task of completing his scheme, Ragged Dick to the new life that had opened so strangely and amazingly before him.

CHAPTER 9

Billy Bunter's Little Way!

RASH!

"Oh!"

"Ow!"

"You silly owl!" roared Bob Cherry.

"You clumsy ass!" yelled Billy Bunter.

It was a terrific collision.

Bob Cherry had run up the Remove staircase and sprinted into the Remove passage. Bob was generally energetic in his movements and now he was in a hurry. That would not have mattered had the coast been clear.

But just as Bob crossed the landing with a rush, Billy Bunter came scudding out of the Remove passage to the stairs.

Bunter had a bundle under his arm, and he seemed in even a greater hurry than Bob Cherry.

Neither saw the other till it was too late.

They met with a crash, and both of them sat down on the Remove landing, spluttering.

Bob leaned helplessy against the balustrade, almost winded by the terrific impact of William George Bunter. A charge with Bunter's weight behind it was no jest.

Bunter clutched at his big spectacles with one hand, with the other at his bundle, which he dropped as he sat down.

"You—you—you silly chump!" he spluttered. "You—you

mad bull! You rhinoceros! What did you charge me over for?"

"You Owl!" gasped Bob. "What did you rush into me for like a blind walrus?"

"You chump!"

"You fat dummy!"

Billy Bunter staggered to his feet, having set his spectacles straight on his fat little nose. Clutching his bundle, he rolled on to the stairs, leaving the hapless Bob still gasping on the landing.

Two juniors came along the Remove passage from Study No. 4 – Vernon Smith and Tom Redwing. Smithy stopped to glance at Bob, and grinned.

"Anything broken?" he asked.

"Ow!"

Bob Cherry staggered to his feet, panting. He leaned on the balustrade to get his breath.

"I'll–I'll burst that fat bounder!" he gasped. "What the thump was he rushing about for, when he can't see a yard from his silly nose? Ow!"

Bob went panting along the Remove passage, and Vernon-Smith and Redwing descended the staircase, laughing. As a matter of fact, the collision had been as much Bob's fault as Bunter's, though Bob did not seem to see it for the moment.

Bob Cherry had recovered his good-humour, however, and almost his breath, by the time he reached his study, No.13 in the Remove.

He hurled open the study door in his usual energetic way, and tramped in with his heavy tread.

Study No. 13 was vacant. It was a half-holiday at Greyfriars, and a sunny afternoon. Most of the Remove fellows were out-of-doors, in the fields or on the river. Harry Wharton & Co. were taking a boat out that afternoon, and four members of the Famous Five were waiting below for Bob.

Bob crossed the study to the cupboard and threw the door

open.

Then he jumped.

On the cupboard shelf there should have been visible a large plum cake, which had arrived from home for Bob that day. That plum cake was to accompany the Famous Five in their pull up the river. By the time they had pulled a few miles up the Sark it was probable that they would be able to do it full justice. Bob Cherry had left it there safe in the cupboard – at all events, it ought to have been safe. Apparently, however, it had not been so safe as he had supposed. For it was no longer there!

"Gone!"

Bob stared into the cupboard. He moved two or three articles to make sure that the cake had not been shoved out of sight by one of his study-mates – Linley or Hurree Singh or Wun Lung. But it was not there. That big plum cake, which was to have furnished a feast for five on the river, had vanished – gone from his gaze like a beautiful dream!

"Bunter!" roared Bob.

He guessed now why the Owl of the Remove had been fleeing out of the Remove passage in such a terrific hurry. He guessed what was in the bundle Bunter had been carrying.

"The–the–the fat villain!" gasped Bob.

He rushed out of the study.

Two or three Remove fellows dodged out of his way in a great hurry as Bob Cherry came speeding back to the staircase.

He went down the stairs three at a time.

Harry Wharton and Johnny Bull, Frank Nugent and Hurree Jamset Ram Singh were waiting for him at the foot of the staircase.

"Hallo, you've been quick, old man!" said Wharton. "But where's the cake? You don't seem to have brought it?"

"Bunter!" gasped Bob.

"What about Bunter?"

"Did you see him? Has he passed you?"

"Yes, five minutes ago!" said Harry. "He went out of the House. He was in rather a hurry, I think!"

"He didn't stop to answer when I asked him what he had got in his bundle," grinned Frank Nugent.

"The cake!" roared Bob.

"What?"

"It's gone — and Bunter — "

"Oh, my hat!"

"After him!" shouted Johnny Bull.

"Come on!" panted Bob.

The Famous Five rushed out into the quadrangle. They stared round for William George Bunter, but William George was not to be seen. Peter Todd was sunning himself on the steps, and Bob caught him by the arm.

"Seen Bunter?"

"Lots of times," answered Peter cheerily. "Oftener than I've wanted to. Don't jerk my arm off!"

"Where did he go?"

"I think he went down to the gates. What's the row?"

Without stopping to explain what the "row" was, Harry Wharton & Co. sprinted down to the gates. It was very probable that Billy Bunter had gone outside the school to seek some secluded spot where he could devour his plunder undisturbed. Gosling was taking the air outside his lodge, and Johnny Bull shouted to him.

"Has Bunter gone out, Gosling?"

"Yes, Master Bull."

"Which way did he go?"

"I think he went towards Courtfield, Master Bull."

"Come on, you fellows!"

And the Co. rushed out of the gates and sped on the road towards Courtfield in towering wrath. There was a severe reckoning in store for the Owl of the Remove — if he was caught!

CHAPTER 10

Bunter Asks For It!

"SMITHY, old man!"

"Cut!"

"I say, Smithy – "

"Hook it," said the Bounder tersely.

"I say, Redwing – "

"Nothing doing, Bunter!" said Tom Redwing, with a smile. "It's Smithy's car, not mine."

"Smithy, old chap – "

"Go and eat coke!"

Vernon–Smith's manner was uncompromising. Billy Bunter's little round eyes glittered behind his spectacles.

At a short distance from the gates of Greyfriars, hidden from the old school by a bunch of beeches, a handsome car was drawn up to the side of the road. Herbert Vernon-Smith and Tom Redwing had walked along to it from the school gates, and they were about to step in when Billy Bunter arrived on the scene, in full and breathless flight, with his precious bundle under his fat arm.

Bunter was in terror of pursuit – a terror that was well-founded. And the sight of Smithy's car was like a windfall to him. Smithy, who had heaps of money to spend, had evidently hired that car for a drive that sunny afternoon with his chum; and Bunter instantly decided that he was going on a motor-

73

drive also. Bunter liked motoring, and, still more, he wanted to get out of the reach of Bob Cherry with his plunder. Smithy's car was, from Bunter's point of view, the right thing in the right place at the right moment.

"I say, you fellows, I'll come," said Bunter. "I'll tell you what – I've got a cake from home, and I'll whack it out with you chaps. I've got it here."

"Whose cake?" grinned the Bounder.

"Mine!" howled Bunter. "It came specially by post this morning, from Bunter Court. Is it a go?"

"My dear ass, I wouldn't have your company for a dozen cakes – even if it was your cake! Buzz off!"

The chauffeur was starting the engine, and Smithy signed to his chum to get into the car. Tom Redwing stepped in.

"I say, Smithy – "

"Rats!"

"Beast!"

"Same to you, old fat man, and many of them! Good-bye!"

"Right-ho, you rotters! I'll tell Wingate you're going out of bounds!" yelled Bunter. "I know your game, Smithy – going to the races on a half-holiday. You've not got leave to go in a car, I know that jolly well!"

"Why, you fat duffer – " began Tom Redwing indignantly.

Vernon-Smith looked back at Bunter, pausing with one foot on the car.

"You think I'm going out of bounds?" he asked.

Bunter sniffed.

"I jolly well know you are!" he answered.

"And you'll mention it to the prefect?"

"Not if you treat me as a pal, old chap," said Bunter affectionately. "I know you'd like me to come."

"So I would on second thoughts," said Smithy. "Hop in! You don't mind, Tom?"

"Not at all, if you don't," answered Redwing.

"The fact is, I want Bunter to come as he puts it so nicely," said the Bounder, with a lurking grin. "Hop in Bunter!"

"Right you are, old chap."

Bunter rolled victoriously into the car, and sat down. Vernon-Smith slammed the door and sat down also, and the car moved. It was a good engine, and it was soon racing away on the road to Courtfield. Billy Bunter cast an anxious glance back as it raced. Far in the distance he discerned five specks on the the white road, and grinned. He guessed that those five specks were the Famous Five of the Remove in wrathful but unavailing pursuit of the captured cake.

Billy Bunter proceeded to unwrap his bundle on his fat knees. A large plum cake was disclosed. Tom Redwing uttered an exclamation.

"That looks like Bob Cherry's cake!" he said.

"Cakes look alike, of course," said Bunter hastily. "This one came specially for me from Bunter Court this morning."

The Bounder chuckled.

"And they wrote Cherry's name on it by mistake?" he asked.

"Eh?"

The Bounder pointed to the paper in which the cake had been wrapped. The name and address of Robert Cherry, of Greyfriars School, were plainly discernible there.

"Oh!" ejaculated Bunter.

Redwing glanced back from the car.

"Why, there's Bob!" he exclaimed. "Bob and the others — they're after Bunter and that cake, Smithy! Stop the car!"

"Don't stop!" roared Bunter in alarm.

Vernon-Smith grinned.

"Bunter's going to give us away for going out of bounds," he said. "We've got to be careful how we handle Bunter."

"Look here, Smithy — "

"Yes, rather," said Bunter. "You'll jolly well get a licking, Smithy! You keep on."

Vernon-Smith signalled to the chauffeur, and the car

slowed down. The five running figures on the road came nearer.

Harry Wharton & Co. had sighted the car, and the gleam of Bunter's spectacles in the sunshine. They were running their hardest, and shouting to Smithy to stop; but the buzz of the car drowned their voices.

"I say, you fellows, I'm going to whack out this cake, of course," said Bunter. "It's my cake, you know — our cook at Bunter Court makes ripping cakes and this is one of them. I don't know how Cherry's name came to be on the paper — "

"Chuck it!" exclaimed Tom Redwing, in disgust. "Look here, Smithy, that's Bob's cake — "

"We're slowing down!" grinned Smithy.

Bunter gave a yell of alarm.

"Beast! I tell you — "

"My dear ass, we're not going to become accessories after the fact in a giddy burglary!" chuckled the Bounder. "Drop the bundle out of the car."

"Shan't!" howled Bunter.

"Then we'll stop."

"I—I say, Smithy — "

The Bounder shrugged his shoulders.

"It's a ripping cake!" urged Bunter. "Look here — "

"Hallo, hallo, hallo!" The Famous Five were near enough now for Bob Cherry's powerful voice to be heard. "Smithy! Stop, there's a good chap! Bunter — "

"Keep on!" shrieked Bunter.

The Bounder laughed.

Bunter blinked back along the road. Harry Wharton & Co. were quite near now, running hard in the dusty wake of the car, which had slowed almost to a crawl.

The Owl of the Remove quaked.

Overtaken by the rightful possessor of the cake, he had not only the loss of his plunder to expect; he had also to expect to be yanked out of the car and thumped and bumped.

"Are you going to drop it?" chuckled Smithy.

"Beast!"

"Take your choice!"

Bunter groaned.

The loss of the cake was better than the loss of the car, with a thumping and bumping thrown in.

With an anguish that could not have been expressed in words, the Owl of the Remove dropped the captured cake over the back of the car. It dropped into the road, and Vernon-Smith signalled at once to the chauffeur to accelerate. The car flew again; and the three occupants, looking back, saw Harry Wharton & Co. come to a breathless halt round the cake.

The car turned from the Courtfield road, into the long country road that led to Lantham. Billy Bunter leaned back in his seat, and blinked in speechless wrath and indignation at the Bounder.

"You awful beast – my cake – " gasped Bunter, finding his voice at last.

"I've got you out of a licking!" grinned Smithy.

"Yah!"

Bunter sat glowering while the car ate up the miles. Really, Smithy's car had not been such a windfall as he had supposed. But he remembered that the Bounder was accustomed to doing things in style when he engaged a car for one of his half-holiday runs; and he cheered up again.

"I say, Smithy, I suppose we're having tea out?" he remarked.

"We are!" assented the Bounder, with a nod.

"A decent feed, I hope?" hinted Bunter.

"Quite decent."

"What's the programme?" asked Bunter, leaning back on the cushions and blinking quite affably at Smithy through his big spectacles. After all, what did the cake matter if he was going to enjoy one of Smithy's expensive feeds at a country hotel after a ripping run in the motor? In the circumstances Bob Cherry was welcome to his own cake — almost.

"We're going through Lantham," said the Bounder. "We stop in Lantham for a few minutes. After that, a straight run on to Canterbury."

"Good!"

"A toppin' tea at Canterbury — the best that can be dug up for love or money — "

"Ripping!"

"Then a run round the country, and a look at the sea, and home to Greyfriars just in time for call-over," said the Bounder.

"Smithy, old man, you're a prince!" said Bunter. "I always liked you, Smithy."

"Let's hope that will continue," said the Bounder cordially. "You're such a nice chap to know, Bunter."

Tom Redwing eyed his comrade curiously. Smithy's dealings with Bunter that sunny afternoon puzzled him a little. But he made no remark, and the rapid car ate up the miles to Lantham. That town, with its railway junction, came in sight in a very short time.

The car slowed down in the streets, and stopped at the railway station.

Vernon-Smith jumped out.

"Come on, Bunter!"

"Eh? What are we getting down for?" asked Bunter.

"Get down and I'll tell you, fathead!"

Bunter rather reluctantly detached himself from the comfortable, cushioned seat, and stepped out of the car. Vernon-Smith pushed him aside with a rather heavy push and stepped into the car again and closed the door. Bunter staggered, and turned towards the car again in amazement. The Bounder regarded him with a cheery grin.

"I—I say, Smithy — "

"Goodbye, old fat man!"

"What?" yelled Bunter.

"You see, dear man, we're not going out of bounds this afternoon," explained Smithy sweetly. "I've got special leave from Mr. Quelch to go on a run to Canterbury to-day. See? So you can tell all the prefects at Greyfriars – Wingate, Walker, Loder, and the whole shoot – tell 'em as often as you like and as long as they'll listen. You can tell Mr. Quelch and the Head – and all the rest of the giddy staff, if you want to. You can tell Gosling and Trotter if you choose. You can shout it from the giddy housetops; you can mention it in Gath, and whisper it in the streets of Askelon. See?"

Bunter blinked.

Tom Redwing burst into a chuckle. The expression on Bunter's fat face at that moment was worth, so to speak, a guinea a box.

"I didn't bring you along because I was afraid you would sneak, old pippin," continued the Bounder. "I brought you along to land you at Lantham, and give you a walk home, for your thundering cheek! See?"

"Ha, ha, ha!" roared Redwing.

The expression on Bunter's face was still more entertaining now. He had been under the impression that he had forced Smithy to take him on board. Smithy's explanation enlightened him on that point – and dismayed him. He blinked at Smithy in blank dismay.

"If you've got the tin you can go home by railway – change at Courtfield!" chuckled the Bounder. "As I know you haven't got any tin – as usual – you can walk. It's about ten miles by the road to – "

"Oh, really, Smithy – "

"But if you know the short cuts you can save a few miles. Anyhow, the walk will do you good. It will bring down your fat, you know; and it may impress on you that I'm a rather bad customer to threaten. Good-bye!"

"Beast! I'm coming!"

"I think not! Get on!" said Vernon-Smith to the chauffeur. The car moved on.

Billy Bunter clung desperately to the handle of the door. The Bounder reached over, and Bunter gave a yell as his hat was squashed on his head. He sat down on the pavement, roaring, and the car glided away.

"Oh, dear! Ow!"

Bunter staggered up.

He blinked after the car; it was fast disappearing in the traffic of Lantham High Street. A minute more and it was gone.

Bunter stood and blinked in overwhelming dismay. He was landed at Lantham. Railway fares were high; but had they been low it would have been all the same to Bunter, as he was in his usual stony state. As usual, his long-expected postal-order had failed to arrive from Bunter Court. If the railway company had been prepared to carry Bunter home for three-pence. Bunter could not have availed himself of the offer. He was fairly landed – and that, so far, was all he had gained by the raid on Bob Cherry's cake and by butting into Smithy's car – and undoubtedly it was all that he deserved.

CHAPTER 11

Wet!

" **H**ALLO, hallo, hallo! Here's the giddy cake, anyhow!"
"Good!"

Harry Wharton & Co. were breathless after their race.
Bob Cherry picked up the cake from the dusty road – it was
intact. Bunter had not had time to take a single bite.

"Well, we've got the cake," said Frank Nugent, laughing.
"Bunter ought to be jolly well bumped; but we've got the
cake!"

"The bumpfulness ought to be terrific," remarked Hurree
Jamset Ram Singh. "But we have got the cake, and it is all
right rainfully."

"Ha, ha, ha!"

The chums of the Remove turned back along the road,
Bob with the cake in its wrappings under his arm. They walked
down to the school raft by the boathouse, where their boat
was waiting for them.

Greyfriars faded into the distance behind as the Famous
Five pulled on between green, wooded banks.

It was a glorious afternoon, and Harry Wharton & Co.
enjoyed the pull up the river.

Some miles from the school they pulled into the bank and
landed on the tow-path under the shade of thick trees, and
the good things – including the recaptured cake – were

landed. The spirit-stove was set going, and the tin kettle set on it, and Bob Cherry brewed coffee.

"This is something like!" remarked Bob, as he sat down in the grass.

"The likefulness is terrific," agreed Hurree Jamset Ram Singh.

"It's a jolly good cake!" said Nugent.

"Hear, hear!"

"Hallo, hallo, hallo! Here comes a cheery-looking merchant! I've seen that chap before somewhere," said Bob.

The juniors glanced at the man who came loafing along the tow-path. He was not a pleasant person to look at – in ragged, dirty clothes, with a battered hat on the back of his untidy head. His face, which looked as if it had not been washed for several weeks, was surly and vicious in expression. A shabby pack which he carried over his shoulder indicated that he was a pedlar – though from his looks it seemed more probable that the pedlar's pack was a pretence, more likely to contain stolen goods than articles for sale.

The juniors eyed him as he slouched up to the camp. The man's dirty, ill-favoured, stubbly face was familiar to them.

"I remember him," said Harry Wharton quietly. "It's that brute who calls himself Pedlar Parker. You remember we came on him that day we went to Compton Woods. He was pitching into a kid – "

"Ragged Dick!" said Bob. "I remember. I wonder what became of that kid?"

"Goodness knows! I hope that brute never got hold of him again!" said Harry.

"He's not with him now, anyhow."

Pedlar Parker came loafing up, and stopped to stare at the schoolboys sitting in the grass under the trees. They recognised him easily enough, but he did not seem to know them again.

" 'Elp a cove on his way?" he said gruffly.

"Certainly!" said Bob. "I'll help you with my boot, with

pleasure, if you're in want of help."

"The helpfulness will be terrific, my esteemed and disgusting scoundrel!" said Hurree Singh.

The man stared at them savagely.

"Ain't got a civil word for a bloke, eh?" he grunted.

"Not for you," said Harry Wharton. "You don't seem to remember us; but we remember you, Mr. Parker."

"Ain't see'd you afore that I know of," growled the ruffian, staring at the captain of the Remove.

"We gave you some reason to remember us," chuckled Bob Cherry. "We handled you for walloping a kid at Compton Woods, and we kept you safe while the kid got away. Remember now?"

Pedlar Parker's eyes glinted.

"So you're that lot, are you?" he said. "You 'elped young Dick to get away, you did, and I ain't see'd him since."

"All the better for him."

Pedlar Parker laid down his pack in the grass. He had a thick knobbly stick under his arm, and he slid it into his hand, with a very ugly expression on his face. The juniors jumped up, quite understanding that the ruffian meant mischief.

"You 'andled me, you did!" said Pedlar Parker. "If I'd 'ad this 'ere stick in my 'and you wouldn't have done it so easy. Now it's my turn!"

"Go ahead!" said Bob Cherry cheerily. Bob had the boathook in his hand, ready for trouble.

"Shell out!" said Pedlar Parker. "I'll let you off for two quid."

Bob Cherry laughed.

The Pedlar glanced up and down the towpath. It was a lonely spot shut in between the woods and the river. There was no one in sight in any direction.

Then he whirled up the heavy cudgel and rushed at the juniors. Undoubtedly the ruffian expected them to scatter before that savage rush, and to knock them right and left with his cudgel. But the Greyfriars fellows were made of sterner stuff than he expected.

There was a crash as Bob's boathook met the cudgel, warding off a savage slash, and the next moment the boathook jabbed on Mr. Parker's ragged waistcoat.

"Ow!" howled the pedlar.

It was quite a painful jab, and it made the ruffian sit down in the grass with a sudden bump.

The next instant the Famous Five were upon him.

Johnny Bull jerked away his cudgel and sent it whirling far out into the river. Mr. Parker rolled in the grass, struggling in the hands of five active fellows.

"Duck him!" shouted Bob.

"Chuck him in!"

"Leggo!" yelled Pedlar Parker. "I'll out yer! I will on my davy I'll out yer! Ow! Ooooooooch!"

Splash!

With a terrific splash the ruffian went headlong into the shallow water amid the reeds and rushes.

He disappeared from sight for a moment, and then came up, spluttering and gasping.

"Ha, ha, ha!"

"Grooogh! Oooooch!"

"It's time you had a wash, old bean!" roared Bob Cherry.

"Ha, ha, ha!"

"Ooooch! Grooogh! Gug-gug-gug!" Pedlar Parker spat out water and mud. "I—I—I'll — Grooogh! Let a bloke get out, blow yer!"

Bob Cherry lunged with the boathook as the ruffian strove to clamber out of the water. Pedlar Parker backed promptly, with the river up to his armpits.

"Ow! Keep off!" he yelled. "Do you want to drown a bloke?"

"It wouldn't be much loss!" grinned Bob.

"Lemme out!" yelled Parker.

"Dear man, you want a wash, and you're getting it. Are you going to 'out' us, as you express it with native eloquence?" chuckled Bob.

"Ow! I'll let you off! I'll clear — on my davy, I will! Let a bloke get out of this 'ere blooming water!" gasped the pedlar.

"Are you sorry?"

"Ow! I—I'll — "

"You're going to stay there till you're properly sorry, old bean!" said Bob, lunging again as the pedlar approached the bank.

"Ow! I'm sorry!" howled Pedlar Parker.

"Are you awfully sorry?"

"I—I—I'll—yes, blow yer!"

"Are you awfully, fearfully sorry?"

"Groogh! Yes! Anything! Let a bloke out!"

"If he's awfully fearfully sorry I think we can let him off, you chaps!" said Bob. "You can come out, you rotter. We'll give you one minute to get clear — or you go in again."

"Ow!"

Pedlar Parker crawled out of the river.

He gave the Greyfriars juniors a venomous look, grabbed up his pack, and tramped away down the towpath, squelching out water as he went. The ducking had taken all the truculence out of the ruffian, and it was evident that he did not want any more trouble with the heroes of Greyfriars. Bob Cherry sat down in the grass again as the pedlar disappeared.

"Pass the cake, Franky."

And the cake was demolished to the last crumb and the last plum, with general satisfaction.

CHAPTER 12

Ragged Dick in a New Role!

RAGGED DICK sat in the corner seat in the railway carriage, looking out with thoughtful, almost wondering eyes at the trees and fields as they flew past the windows of the express.

Ragged Dick!

That was what he had been called in his days on the road, but the nickname seemed a ludicrous misnomer now.

Dick was no longer ragged. He was well-dressed – even expensively dressed. He carried his clothes well, too. In the quadrangle at Greyfriars he would have passed muster with the best.

He was not used to it yet. Even now he wondered sometimes whether it was not all a dream, whether he would not wake up under a hedge or a haystack, with the coarse, harsh voice of Pedlar Parker cursing in his ears, or hearing the drunken ramblings of Spouting Billy.

Ragged, nameless, friendless, forlorn only a few short weeks ago. And now –

It did not seem real. Ragged Dick had become Richard Compton, grandson by adoption of Sir Henry Compton, of Compton Hall. All that wealth could give him was his – and the dearest ambition of his life, an ambition he had never hoped to realise, was about to become a fact. He was going to school, to Greyfriars, where his keen desire to study and learn would be taken as a matter of course, instead of being the mockery and derision of the rough characters with whom he had associated on the road.

He stole a glance at the tall, stern-faced rather grim-looking old gentleman on the opposite seat.

Sir Henry Compton was reading his newspaper, oblivious of his adopted grandson.

His hard, brown face was grim in expression; nobody, looking at the old baronet, would have dreamed that he had a kind or tender heart.

Yet why had he done this for the nameless waif? Why had he taken into his charge, and given his ancient and honoured name to, the ragged, tattered lad who had trespassed in his park?

It was a mystery to Ragged Dick.

Why should the old man care anything for him? Indeed, he had shown no sign of caring anything for him. His manner was not unkind in dealing with the boy; but it could not be called kind. No affectionate word ever passed his lips; and he addressed the lad as Richard when he spoke to him – never by any chance "Dick."

Why had he done this – lifted the hapless waif from the underworld, and placed him in a position that crowds of fellows – even Greyfriars fellows – might well have envied?

Dimly at the back of Dick's mind was a misgiving – so faint that he hardly realised it; yet it was there. The baronet had had some motive – and that motive was not regard for the boy personally – it could not be that, and it was not that. Yet the motive must exist. If the old man, childless since his only son had died, desired to adopt someone to carry on his ancient name, he would naturally have chosen a relative. If he, indeed, had no relatives, which seemed incredible, surely he would have chosen someone in his own rank in society – someone better fitted by birth and training to carry on the traditions of the Comptons, than poor Dick could ever be.

Was there something more behind it?

Ragged Dick had wondered about it – he could not help wondering. Perhaps his secret misgiving was chiefly caused by the secrecy of the affair. He had been taken to London – the only servant at Compton Hall who had seen him had been sent to the baronet's estate in Scotland to keep him out of the way. Dick was not to be seen at the Hall until the school holidays came round, and then he was to appear as Richard Compton; not the adopted grandson, but the genuine grandson of the old landowner.

Why?

Was Sir Henry one of those who do good by stealth, and blush to find it fame? Why was the adoption to be kept so profoundly secret. To avoid chatter and comment? Certainly Sir Henry was the kind of man to dislike anything of that kind. Was that it?

But if Dick was to appear as the grandson of the baronet, there must have been a grandson in existence at some time— all Compton Hall would know whether Sir Henry's dead son had left a boy behind him or not. And back into Ragged Dick's mind would come the remembrance of the strange scene in Compton Park, when the old man had muttered the word "Dead" after reading the telegram, and had fallen in a seizure. Had the grandson died, and was Dick taken in his place? It seemed so – yet why?

These questions were never quite out of the boy's mind; but generally they were rather at the back of his mind. He knew Sir Henry's wishes, and loyally meant to carry them out. Sir Henry had bidden him ask no questions; and he asked none. Sir Henry had bidden him keep his adoption a secret, and act and speak as though he really were Richard Compton, and it was for Sir Henry to decide upon that point. Dick had not the remotest idea of gainsaying him. Perplexed as he was, it never crossed his mind, even vaguely or remotely, that there could be anything wrong, anything illegal, in what the baronet was doing. That he was made heir to an entailed estate, which, by law, should go to the heir-in-entail at the old baronet's death, was a suspicion that was not likely to occur to him. That the baronet was at bitter feud with his cousin Roger, the spendthrift and gambler, and determined to keep an unmitigated blackguard out of Compton Hall, by fair means or foul, Dick was not likely to guess – he had never even heard of Roger Compton.

The mystery puzzled him, when he thought of it; but it did not trouble his spirits.

He was happy – there was no doubt about that.

This day he was going to Greyfriars – Sir Henry Compton had previously arranged matters with Dr. Locke, the headmaster. Now he was taking him to the school. All the Comptons had been Greyfriars men since there had been Comptons in Kent, and Greyfriars had had a local habitation and a name. Long, long since old Sir Henry himself had been in the Remove – the Form which Dick was to enter.

Dick's heart was light as he turned from his contemplation of the grim old face of Sir Henry, and stared at the scenery again. Fields and woods – the glorious scenery of the Garden of England – passed before his eyes; in the distance a spire showed that they were nearing Lantham.

An hour or so more and he would be at Greyfriars.

He wondered what the fellows would be like. He wondered whether any of them would suspect that the wealthy well-dressed newcomer had ever been other than what he now seemed.

It was not likely.

Ragged Dick was not a conceited fellow, but he knew that he looked the part well enough. And he had only to hold his tongue – and that he was bound to do by his patron's instructions and by the solemn promise he had made.

BILLY BUNTER'S TRAMP!

Compton Hall, in the far distance, flashed by the train. Under those ancient red roofs was to be his future home – under those old trees he had first met the baronet and helped him when he lay mumbling and groaning in the seizure which had followed the reading of the telegram. In the fields close by he had been beaten by Pedlar Parker – he remembered how a crowd of schoolboys had intervened to rescue him from the brute, and how, in his eagerness to escape from his tyrant, he had fled without even a word of thanks.

If ever he met those fellows again – But he smiled at the thought. It was not likely that he would meet them – not likely that he would know them again if he did. Still more unlikely that they would know him – the ragged, dirty, unwashed tramp transformed into the clean and well-dressed young gentleman.

His life had been strange enough, but this was the strangest of all. Long, long ago – so long ago in infancy that the memory was dim and blurred – he had had a father, like other fellows. What had become of him, whether he still lived even, Dick did not know. His next recollection was of tramping the roads with a gipsy van and a gipsy gang. Older, he had run away from the gipsies, and then had come his tramping with Poynings, the fallen Master of Arts, who had taught him in his sober hours most of what he knew, and in his drunken hours sometimes cursed and beaten him.

After that he wandered alone, till he had thrown in his lot with Pedlar Parker. And then had followed weeks of ill-usage because he would not "pinch," as the ruffian called it, Ragged Dick looking all the time for an opportunity of escape from his tyrant – an opportunity that had come the day the unknown schoolboys had chipped in to help him.

After that – the meeting with Sir Henry in Compton Park, and the strangest of all the many changes in his young life. The weeks in London had passed like a strange dream – the visits to the tailors and the outfitters, the days of "grinding" with a tutor who had prepared him to take his place in the Lower Fourth Form at Greyfriars. The tutor had known nothing of him save that he was Sir Henry's grandson, who had been in delicate health and whose education had been a little neglected; but his pupil had rather surprised him by the extent of his knowledge of some things, the extent of his ignorance of others. Spouting Billy, in his sober moments, had been a good teacher.

Even now, as the spire of Lantham Church grew nearer against the blue summer sky, and Greyfriars seemed quite close at hand, Ragged Dick wondered whether it was not all a dream.

The train slowed down, and the hard voice of the old baronet broke in upon his musings.

"Richard!"

Dick started. He was getting used to being called Richard now, but it was still a little strange to him.

"Yes, sir."

"We change at Lantham in a few minutes. There will be a quarter of an hour to wait for the train to Courtfield."

"Yes."

Dick answered quietly, submissively. He was awed, sometimes almost scared, by the grim old gentleman whose grandson he was supposed to be.

"I shall wait in the station; you may take a walk in the town if you choose. You will return in good time for the train."

"Yes, sir."

Dick understood that Sir Henry did not desire his company during the wait at Lantham. He wondered whether the old man was absolutely indifferent to him, for whom he had done so much. It seemed so.

The express halted.

Sir Henry stepped out, tall and stately and icy. Dick followed him from the carriage. He was a sturdy fellow, but he felt strangely small as he walked by the side of the tall gentleman.

Sir Henry entered a waiting-room.

"Return here in ten minutes, Richard."

"Yes, sir."

"Use your eyes, Richard. As my grandson you may be supposed to know something of the neighbourhood in which you lived in childhood."

"Oh!"

"You may go, Richard!" said the baronet coldly.

Dick walked down the platform.

Sir Henry Compton stared after him, with a kind of grim approval in his face. The boy was handsome, well-set-up, decent. He was no Compton, but he would do credit to the name that had been given him. Sir Henry did not repent of the sudden resolution he had taken after his hostile interview with his cousin, the spendthrift blackguard — the waster and rogue from whose wasteful hands this boy was to save the old Compton lands and the old Hall. Grim and hard and obstinate, the old man was not given to repenting of any wilful decision to which he might come.

He sat down in the waiting-room, and Dick — unconsciously lighter of heart out of the old man's icy company — walked out of the station, his handsome face cheery and bright.

CHAPTER 13

A Surprise for Billy Bunter!

BILLY BUNTER groaned.

From the dismal depths of his fat circumference came that groan, expressive of his dismal feelings.

Smithy's car had vanished. The Bounder and Tom Redwing were far away on their joy ride to Canterbury. And Billy Bunter stood alone, wrapped in dismay as in a garment.

He was hungry. That alone was a very serious matter – a matter, indeed, of which the seriousness transcended the seriousness of all other matters in the earth, in the air, or in the waters under the earth.

There was a cafe opposite the station at Lantham – there was a restaurant at the corner. But these establishments were not run on Good Samaritan lines. They succoured the hungry and thirsty only for cash payment – and Bunter was minus cash. He might as well have been in the middle of the Sahara Desert, so far as his chances of obtaining refreshment went. Water, indeed was supplied free at the fountain in the market-place, but that was of no use to Bunter. He did not like water inside, and disliked it intensely outside. It was not like the sad case of the Ancient Mariner, with "water, water everywhere, nor any drop to drink." It was with Bunter a case of provender all around, nor any morsel to eat. Which was a sadder case – at least, in Bunter's estimation.

BILLY BUNTER'S TRAMP!

Famished as he was — for it was two hours since dinner, when he had eaten only enough for three — there was no hope of sustenance until he got back to Greyfriars. Walking was impossible, for walking meant exertion. Railway travelling might have seemed impossible to any other fellow without cash in his pockets. Not so Bunter. He was prepared to bilk the railway company for a ride. The only question was whether the railway company could be bilked.

He heard the roar of an incoming express in the station, and knew that the London train was in. He was aware that London passengers had to change if they wanted to go on to Courtfield, so there would be a train for that town before very long. He rolled into the station, hoping to sneak upon the platform in the slack time between two trains, then to dodge into the Courtfield coaches without a ticket. As for what would happen when he arrived at Courtfield ticketless, that had to remain on the knees of the gods. Bunter was accustomed to trusting to luck in such little matters. It was useless to meet trouble half-way. The immediate problem was to get on the platform undetected by meddlesome porters and guards.

Passengers by the express were coming out by one gate, and another, giving access to the Courtfield platform, was open. Bunter rolled towards it with an elaborate air of carelessness. He stooped to tie a shoe-lace, he stopped to stare at a poster which announced the glories of Blackpool for summer holidays, he loafed round an automatic machine. Inch by inch, as it were, he approached the open gate, and rolled in.

But alas for Bunter!

A station official emerged from behind a trolley, and a heavy hand dropped on Bunter's shoulder.

"Ticket, please!"

Bunter's fat heart thumped.

He turned an indignant blink on the porter. What right had

the fellow to put a hand on his shoulder – the shoulder of a public-school chap, too! As a matter of fact, the Lantham porter had had an amused eye on Bunter for some minutes, and was quite aware that he was seeking to steal a ride.

"Ticket, sir!"

"Leggo! I mean, wait a minute! I've got it here!"

Bunter fumbled in his pockets.

The porter waited, grinning derisively. He had been there before, so to speak – he knew the manners and customs of a bilk. He was not at all surprised when the fat junior finally announced:

"Oh, dear! I've dropped it somewhere!"

"Thought you 'ad, sir!" assented the man. "Sort of guessed it, sir! You looked like it!"

"I don't want any impertinence, my man!" said Bunter, with an attempt at bluster.

"I daresay!" assented the Lantham man. "I don't want any bilking, if you come to that. I've seen your sort afore, I 'ave! You just stand there, sir, while I call a copper to 'elp you find that there ticket you've dropped."

The porter turned away.

The instant his back was turned Billy Bunter scudded away from the gate, plunging across the station vestibule towards the street. And the Lantham porter chuckled, and gave no further heed.

The Owl of the Remove was baffled. After that attempt he was not likely to make a further essay at bilking that afternoon. He was only too glad to get clear without a personal interview with the "copper" the Lantham man had mentioned.

He rolled out of the station hurriedly. A blink behind assuring him that he was not pursued, he stopped to take breath. What was he going to do? That was the question. Or, to put it more accurately, whom was he going to do? Something or somebody had to be done, that was certain.

BILLY BUNTER'S TRAMP!

Passengers by the express from London were leaving the station – and Bunter, as he noticed them, was struck by a happy thought. He was aware that a new fellow was coming to Greyfriars that afternoon – a fellow named Compton, who was going into the Remove. He had heard Mr. Quelch speak of it. New fellows were Bunter's game. New fellows were innocent enough to lend Bunter half-a-crown with the hope of seeing it again; new fellows might even advance a loan on the postal-order that Bunter was expecting – not being acquainted with that celebrated postal-order, like older hands at Greyfriars. This particular new fellow, Compton, would have to change at Lantham if he was coming from London, and if Bunter could get hold of him –

The Owl of the Remove brightened up.

The fellow would have to wait for the Courtfield train – it was not in the station yet. He would be hanging about somewhere. It was only a question of getting in touch with him.

The rest depended. If the fellow looked bright Bunter would simply "touch" him for the fare home, as a Greyfriars chap who had lost his railway ticket and was stranded; but if he looked simple Bunter would tell him the old, old story of the expected postal-order, and extract from him a loan just as extensive as the new fellow's means and simplicity permitted.

Bunter felt quite bucked.

He turned back into the station, to blink about in search of a fellow who looked likely to be a new chap for the school – with one eye warily open for a suspicious porter and a possible copper.

And then Bunter jumped.

Coming out of the station was a fellow of about his own age, though resembling him in no other point.

A handsome, sturdy fellow, extremely well-dressed, with a bright and cheery look. Bunter's spectacles almost fell off as he saw him.

96

He was so astounded that he blinked and blinked again, scarcely able to believe the evidence of his eyes and his big glasses.

Bunter had seen that youth before – seen him when he was not well-dressed and spick-and-span, seen him when he was tattered and dirty and forlorn. He had seen him face to face and talked with him – under the old trees of Compton Park only a few weeks ago. Bunter's vision was not keen, and his memory for faces was not specially good, but he knew that face again in spite of the change in its owner. He knew it well, and beyond the shadow of a doubt.

And standing in the path of the well-dressed youth as he came out of the station, blocking Richard Compton's way with his fat figure, Bunter stared and blinked at him in blank astonishment, and ejaculated :

"Ragged Dick !"

CHAPTER 14

Not Bunter's Lucky Day!

"RAGGED DICK!"

Bunter fairly gasped out the name.

He had never expected to see Ragged Dick again — he had never even thought of him since that meeting in Compton Park. And here was the fellow face to face once more, exhibiting every sign of wealth; the tattered tramp had become a well-dressed youth of the most prosperous appearance. Had Bunter not been a suspicious fellow he might have thought there was something queer about this startling change. And Bunter was not unsuspicious by any means.

"Ragged Dick!" he repeated. "My hat! What a change!"

Dick stared at him.

Like Bunter, he had forgotten that encounter in Compton Park — the fat schoolboy had not lingered in his memory. But he knew him again; Bunter — at least, his circumference — was not easily forgotten.

"You!" said Dick.

Bunter grinned.

"Little me!" he said.

Dick looked at him, expecting apparently that the fat fellow would move and give him room to pass. Bunter did not move, and Dick walked round him and went out of the station.

Bunter was after him like a shot.

Ragged Dick felt himself caught by the arm, and as he looked angrily round he found Bunter's grinning, fat face at his elbow.

"Let go!" he snapped.

"Do you want me to call a policeman?" grinned Bunter.

"A—a policeman?"

"Just that!" chuckled Bunter. "I know you, my pippin! You're the tramp I gave charity to in Compton Park —"

"I'm the chap you insulted, and who floored you," answered Dick. "And I'll floor you again if you don't take your paw off my arm!"

Bunter's fat hand jerked away.

"Look here — "

"Oh, let me alone!" snapped Dick. "I don't want to have anything to say to you. I don't know you, and don't want to!"

"I dare say you don't," agreed Bunter, with a fat chuckle. "But I jolly well know you, and I've a jolly good mind to give you in charge."

"Are you potty?" Dick stared at the fat junior. "How could you give me in charge, you dummy?"

"Where did you get that clobber?"

"This clobber?"

"And that watch and chain!" grinned Bunter. "And those pearl studs! Tramps don't dress like that, my boy! He, he, he!"

Dick stared at him, and his handsome face grew a little troubled. He understood Bunter's astonishment now at seeing him, and he hardly wondered at Bunter's suspicion that he had come by his present possessions dishonestly. The change in his fortunes, which seemed like a dream to himself, was quite unknown to this fellow, of course. Any fellow might have been suspicious, seeing that amazing change in the one-time tattered waif.

For Bunter's opinion and suspicions Dick did not care a jot. But he wanted to keep clear of any fellow who had seen him in his old character. His secret – the secret of Sir Henry Compton had warned him so sternly to keep – was at stake.

He did not answer Bunter; he turned away and strode quickly down the High Street of Lantham.

"Stop!" shouted Bunter.

Dick did not heed; he hurried on. His idea was to shake the fat fellow off and return by another route to the railway-station.

Once he was safe in the train for Greyfriars he would be done with him, and he would be careful not to take another walk in Lantham, where he supposed Bunter belonged.

It did not occur to his mind then that Bunter belonged to Greyfriars – any more than it occurred to Bunter that this fellow, whom he knew as Ragged Dick, was the Richard Compton who was booked to arrive at the school that after-noon with his grandfather.

Bunter had forgotten about the new fellow, upon whose pocket-money he had such deep designs, in his surprise at this unexpected encounter – and in his deep interest in the strangely-changed waif.

He rolled down the street after Dick, shouting to him.

"Stop! Do you hear? Stop!"

Dick paid no heed.

He hurried on, with burning cheeks, keenly conscious of the curious glances turned on him by people he passed. The pursuit was attracting attention.

"Stop!" roared Bunter. "I say, there, stop him!"

Dick halted at last.

He did not want a crowd gathering about him, and he had already attracted more attention from the passers-by than liked.

Billy Bunter came up, panting.

"In a hurry – what?" he grinned.

"You fat fool!" said Dick fiercely. "What do you want?"

"Better language, you cad!"

Dick clenched his fists.

"What do you want?" he repeated. "If you've anything to say, say it and let me alone!"

"Lots!" said Bunter. "I know jolly well where you got those clothes — you pinched them!"

"Is that all?"

"I think I ought to give you in charge!" said Bunter loftily. "You've stolen those clothes and that watch and chain, it stands to reason."

Dick laughed impatiently.

"I've done nothing of the kind."

"Then how did you get hold of them?"

"That's my business!"

"Mine, too, I think!" sneered Bunter. "I've a jolly good mind to call a policeman. Still, if you give me your word that you didn't steal those clothes — "

"Well, I do, if that is what you want."

Bunter grinned.

"Were they given to you?"

"Yes!" said Dick between his teeth.

"I know — given to you by a chap who didn't know it at the time!" chuckled Bunter. "Chap bathing, perhaps, and you came along and annexed his clobber — what? He, he, he!"

Dick smiled involuntarily. Perhaps that was a natural theory, so far as Bunter was concerned, to account for the startling change in his appearance.

"Well, I don't want to be hard on you," said Bunter generously. "I'm a kind-hearted chap. I'll tell you how the matter stands."

"What on earth do you mean?"

"I'm stony!" explained Bunter.

"Stony?" repeated Dick.

"Yes. Can you lend me a quid?"

"No!"

"Think again!" said Bunter. "There's a bobby at the corner.

Think again, old bean!"

Dick stared at him. He did not know Bunter. Any fellow at Greyfriars could have told him that Bunter was a weird mixture of fool and rogue; but Dick had never been at Greyfriars – yet. It was natural, in the circumstances, that he should conclude that Bunter was all rogue – as his remarks certainly seemed to indicate.

"Why you–you scoundrel!" exclaimed Ragged Dick indignantly. "You think I've stolen the money, and you want some of it! You ought to be taken in charge by a policeman yourself, you rascal!"

"What?" roared Bunter.

"You rascal!" exclaimed Dick. "You're no better than a thief, on your own words!"

Bunter fairly spluttered with indignation. He was very far from realising that he was a rascal.

"You cheeky tramp! You–you impertinent waster! You–you are – "

Bunter gasped with rage.

There was a chime from Lantham Church. Ragged Dick started. It was half-past three, and the ten minutes allowed by Sir Henry Compton had more than elapsed. He had no more than time to scud back to the station and catch the train with the baronet.

He stepped back and turned, and Bunter clutched at his arm and stopped him, his fat face red with rage.

"You cheeky rotter!" gasped Bunter. "I'll show you! I'll–"

"Let go!"

"I'll jolly well give you a lesson! I'll–I'll – Yarooooop!" roared Bunter, as he received a hefty shove on his fat chest, and sat down on the pavement. "Oh! Ow! Wow! Groogh! Oh, my hat! Stop! Stop, thief! Ow!"

Ragged Dick, without another glance at the fat junior, was speeding back to the railway station.

Bunter staggered up.

"Ow! Oh dear! I'll jolly well have him arrested! Ow! Wow!" He dusted his clothes, breathing wrath and indignation. "A common fellow like that — a tramp and a thief — shoving a chap over, laying his low hands on a gentleman! Oh dear! Ow! Now I shan't catch that fellow Compton. Oh dear! He will be gone on to Courtfield, if the beast came by that train. Oh, crumbs! Ow!"

Billy Bunter gasped and spluttered, and rolled on breathlessly to the station. But the Courtfield train was gone when he arrived there, and Ragged Dick was gone, and there was nobody to be seen about the station who looked at all likely to be Richard Compton, the new fellow for the Greyfriars Remove. It was not Billy Bunter's lucky afternoon.

CHAPTER 15

Pedlar Parker is Surprised!

"RICHARD!"

"Yes, sir!" gasped Dick.

Ragged Dick arrived breathlessly, and he found Sir Henry Compton waiting for him impatiently with a frowning brow.

"You are late?"

"Yes. I—I— "

"We have one minute for the train," said Sir Henry coldly. "Follow me!"

"Yes," gasped Dick.

The baronet did not speak again till he was seated in the Courtfield train with the boy. Then, as the train rolled out of Lantham, he fixed his eyes on the waif opposite. Dick's face was clouded. He could see that his protector was angry, and it made him troubled and uneasy.

"You were late. You should have returned to the station in ten minutes, as I directed you," said Sir Henry in a hard voice.

"I couldn't help it, sir."

"If the train had been lost I could not have kept my appointment with Dr. Locke, your future headmaster."

"I know, sir. But — "

"You must understand, Richard, that your old life is over for ever. That you are no longer free to consult your own whims and caprices," said Sir Henry. "Your life henceforth will be orderly and disciplined. You will obey the instructions of those set in authority over you, and will refrain from following your own wilful fancies."

Dick crimsoned. The baronet was evidently under the impression that he had wandered thoughtlessly about the Lantham streets, forgetful of the passage of time.

"I know, sir. But it was because — "

Sir Henry raised a brown hand.

"You need not excuse yourself, Richard. I understand. I am only warning you that you must take more care."

"Yes; but — "

"You need say no more."

The baronet opened his newspaper again, and devoted his attention to it.

Ragged Dick said no more.

He had wondered whether it would be wiser to mention his meeting with a fellow who had seen him before as Ragged Dick, but it was plain that Sir Henry desired to hear nothing from him. That the boy had been delayed by no fault of his own had not occurred to the baronet, and he desired to hear no explanations.

Dick said no more. After all, he had done with the fat fellow who had troubled him; he did not expect ever to see him again. It was useless to describe the incident to Sir Henry.

The journey to Courtfield Junction was made in silence, save for the occasional grunt of the baronet, as he came on some item in his newspaper which did not meet with his approval.

Dick stared at the scenery that fleeted by the windows. But he was not thinking of it; he was thinking of Greyfriars School, coming nearer and nearer now. Thinking of the headmaster, unknown so far, but awe-inspiring; of the crowd of fellows he would meet — two or three hundred complete strangers among whom his lot was now to be cast. Perhaps he would make friends there? Why should he not? Fellows who would have stared at the thought of making friends with Ragged Dick would probably be friendly enough with Richard Compton heir of Compton Hall. Dick smiled as he thought of it. The poet has said that the rank is but the guinea's stamp, and the man's the gold, for all that. But the Compton stamp on the tattered waif made a very great deal of difference.

"Courtfield Junction! Changer 'ere for Friardale and Greyfriars!"

The train stopped in the station.

Dick followed Sir Henry down the platform and out into the street. Sir Henry was not taking the local train to Friardale; he signalled to a taxicab. The taxi bowled along the Courtfield road towards Greyfriars, and Ragged Dick's heart beat faster as it went.

The school was close at hand now.

There was a little mirror in the taxi, and Dick looked at his reflection in it. He saw there a handsome face, bright and healthy. Somehow he would not have been surprised to see the reflection of the unwashed face of Ragged Dick of old, so unreal did all this seem to him. Uneasiness grew in his breast. He was going among a crowd of well-dressed fellows, fellows accustomed to the good things of life; fellows who would, perhaps, have sneered superciliously at the tattered waif Dick had been. He grew hot in the cheeks at the thought. Was he not, in a way, an imposter – a fellow pretending to be what he was not? Would he not be justly despised if it should come out what he was – what he had been?

And yet – and yet he was himself, whatsoever might be his outward trappings. In the garments, and with the name of Richard Compton, in a shining silk-hat, and with money in his pocket, he was still the nameless waif; but it was upon his character that all depended. If he made himself liked and respected he would owe it to himself, not to his trappings.

But would he be able to play the part? Would not some keen and suspicious eye detect the tramp in the gentleman's clothes? His heart was beating painfully as a grey old tower rose in the distance over leafy trees.

Sir Henry's stern face relaxed a little.

"That is Greyfriars," he said.

It was his old school, and it had a place in his heart; not a tender heart, but not unfeeling. His glance went to the boy at his side doubtingly. Dick felt that he was being scrutinised, that a doubt was in the baronet's mind whether he would pass muster. His strange way of life had made him quick of observation.

But the old man gave a nod, as if of approval and satisfaction. Dick breathed quickly.

"You—you think I—I shall pass, sir?" he stammered.

Sir Henry's face hardened again.

"I should not have brought you here had I not thought so," he answered coldly.

Dick flushed and was silent. The words, hard as they were, gave him comfort. This was no man who was trying a dubious experiment from motives of kindness. Sir Henry would not have brought him there without the assurance that he would be able to take his place in the Greyfriars crowd. And Sir Henry knew.

Three well-dressed fellows lounged along the road and glanced idly at the taxicab as it whirled by. Dick glanced at them, wondering if they were Greyfriars fellows. As a matter of fact they were Ponsonby and his friends of Highcliffe School. Dick caught a careless word as the taxi passed them.

"That's old Compton."

They were gone.

They had looked at the old baronet, not at Dick. Certainly they had seen nothing to make them suspect that the well-dressed youth in the taxi had once tramped the roads as a nameless, homeless waif. That was little enough, but the troubled boy drew comfort from it.

He caught a glimpse of the river through the trees. There were boats on the water, with schoolboys rowing – these would be Greyfriars fellows, he decided. Two big fellows were coming towards the school from the direction of the boathouse; one had a cane under his arm. They looked like men to Dick. These could not be Greyfriars chaps. They were Wingate and Gwynne of the Sixth if he had known it. The trees hid them again.

The road ran between Greyfriars and the river. On the grass by the roadside a tramp lay with a pack beside him, leaning against a tree, staring before him with evil eyes. Dick felt a throb of pity as he glanced at the tattered figure. This was what he had been – what he still would have been, but for Sir Henry Compton. And then suddenly his heart stood still as he recognised the dirty, evil face. The man who lay in the grass was Pedlar Parker.

He shrank back in the taxi.

If the man saw him –

The evil eyes of the ruffian turned spitefully on the passing vehicle.

Then Pedlar Parker gave a jump.

He leapt to his feet, as the taxi passed, and stood staring after the taxi with amazed eyes.

The man had seen him, recognised him, in spite of the change in him – recognised him as that fat fellow at Lantham had done. By what rotten ill-fortune was Pedlar Parker still tramping in that part of Kent? It was a stroke of cruel luck.

A bend in the road hid the tramp.

The taxi turned in at the gates; Gosling touched his hat with immense respect to Sir Henry Compton.

"Richard, what is the matter with you?" Sir Henry's voice was harsh. "Sit down, boy, and do not look scared!"

"I–I– "

"There is nothing to fear!" snapped the baronet. "Have I

been mistaken in you?"

"But I— "

"That will do. Pull yourself together. You will be in the presence of your headmaster in a few minutes."

Dick sank back in his seat, his heart beating. After all, what was there to fear? Pedlar Parker could not hurt him now — the dirty ruffian would never even venture into the school gates — he dared not. There was nothing to fear — nothing. But his heart was still beating painfully as he was shown, with Sir Henry Compton, into the presence of Dr. Locke, headmaster of Greyfriars.

CHAPTER 16

Compton of the Remove!

"THAT'S the giddy old baronet!"

Bob Cherry made the remark as the chums of the Remove sauntered towards the House.

The tall figure of Sir Henry Compton loomed up coming away from the house.

His interview with the Head and Mr. Quelch finished, Sir Henry's business at Greyfriars was over.

His face was grimly thoughtful as he came out. The taxicab, which had been waiting for him, buzzed up, and Sir Henry stepped into it.

"Compton Hall!" he said to the driver.

He glanced carelessly at the five juniors, and they "capped" him respectfully, the old gentleman slightly acknowledging the salute as the taxi buzzed away down the drive.

"Looks rather a gargoyle, doesn't he?" said Bob. "Sort of jolly old mastiff. I wonder what he's been here for? Some Greyfriars chap been on his land again?"

Wharton shook his head.

"Not this time, I think. There's a Compton kid coming to Greyfriars. Bunter heard about it, and told the Remove passage. I dare say the old chap came to bring him here."

"Oh, yes, I remember! A new kid for the Remove," said Bob. "The jolly old gent's grandson. Lucky young bargee—"

"With a grandfather like that?" asked Nugent. "I don't think I should quite like a chivvy like that around the house!"

Bob chuckled.

"But the kid's in for a good thing – Compton Hall and Compton Park and Compton Woods and an estate in Scotland, and no end of quids," he said, "as well as the jolly old title. A chap might like to change places with young Compton with his grandfather's chivvy thrown in. I dare say the old johnny isn't so jolly ferocious as he looks, too. May be quite a nice man inside."

"I don't know," said Nugent. "There is a lot of yarns told by the local gossips about old Compton. He's hard as nails. He gives poachers jolly stiff sentences when he's on the bench!"

"Well, they shouldn't poach, you know," said Bob tolerantly.

"And it's pretty well known that he's at daggers drawn with his cousin Roger who comes next in the entail after his grandson," said Nugent.

"I've seen that chap!" said Johnny Bull. "I saw him coming back from Courtfield races one day in a car with two or three horsey blighters and too drunk to sit upright."

"My hat! No wonder old Compton doesn't like him, then!" said Bob. "He doesn't look the man to like that sort of thing."

"There's a story about his brother, too," said Nugent. "He had a younger brother and rowed with him, and the chap left the Hall after a frightful scene and has never been there since. He's supposed to be dead now. But I dare say a lot of it is gossip. I wonder what young Compton is like?"

"If he's a chip off the old block he won't be very nice, I fancy!" said Wharton. "Let's hope they won't crowd him into our study."

"Or into mine!" grinned Bob. "We are four in Study No. 13 already. You are only two in Study No. 1, so you're more likely to get him."

"Oh, rotten!" said Nugent.

The Famous Five went into the House, and Wingate of the Sixth called to the captain of the Remove.

"Wharton!"

"Yes, Wingate?"

"Mr. Quelch wants to speak to you in his study."

"Right-ho!"

The Co. went up the stairs, and Harry repaired to his Form-master's study. He found Mr. Quelch alone there.

"Ah! Wharton," said Mr. Quelch, laying down his pen. "I wish to speak to you, Wharton, about a new boy who is entering the Remove. I have decided to place him in your study."

"Yes, sir," said Harry resignedly. He had no prejudice against the new fellow, whom he had never seen — so far as he knew — but he did not want a newcomer in Study No. 1. But that was a matter for his Form-master to decide, and it was for the junior to grin and bear it.

"Doubtless you have heard of Sir Henry Compton, of Compton Hall?" said the Remove-master.

"Yes, sir. I've just passed him," said Harry.

"He brought his grandson here this afternoon. Richard Compton has been in delicate health and has lived abroad under medical care for a long time, I am told," said Mr. Quelch. "Certainly he looks healthy and sturdy enough; but that is what I am told. He seems a very pleasant and well-behaved boy, and I hope you will find him an agreeable companion in your study, Wharton."

"I hope so, sir," said Harry demurely.

"I have sent him to your study, and told him to wait for you there," said Mr. Quelch. "I am sure that you will make him welcome, Wharton."

"I will do my best, sir," said Harry.

"Thank you, Wharton!"

Mr. Quelch returned to his papers again, and the captain of the Remove left his study.

He met Vernon-Smith and Redwing on the stairs as he went up to the Remove passage.

"Bunter come in yet?" asked Smithy.

"Bunter! I haven't seen him," answered Wharton. "Didn't he go for a motor run with you? I saw him in your car."

The Bounder chuckled.

"I dropped him at Lantham, to walk home," he explained. "He thought we were going out of bounds, and threatened to report us to a prefect if we didn't give him a lift to get away with your cake. So I gave him a lift as far as Lantham, and left him there."

Harry Wharton laughed.

"I suppose he's still crawling home," chuckled Smithy. "He will be nearly dead by the time he gets here. Poor old Bunter!"

"It was really rather too bad!" said Tom Redwing, laughing.

"Serve him jolly well right!" said Harry, and he went on up the stairs and into Study No. 1.

"Compton here?" he asked.

"Here he is," answered Frank Nugent. "He says he's going to be in this study."

"Yes, I've just had it from Mr. Quelch."

Wharton glanced rather curiously at the handsome lad who rose from the armchair. Ragged Dick, otherwise Richard Compton, returned his glance with equal curiosity.

"So you're going to be our study-mate, Compton," said Harry, and he held out his hand.

Dick shook hands with him. Wharton's eyes were still lingering on his face.

"I've heard from Mr. Quelch that you've been abroad a lot," he said. "But haven't I met you before somewhere?"

"Not that I know of," answered Dick, looking at him. "But it's rather odd – I seem to have seen your face somewhere."

"I was thinking the same," said Nugent, with a puzzled look. "I seem to have seen Compton somewhere before to-day."

"Well, we've seen his grandfather often enough, and I dare say there's some resemblance. That would be it, I suppose!" said Harry – but he was puzzled.

Dick smiled involuntarily.

There was not likely to be much resemblance between Sir Henry Compton and a grandson by adoption. Not for a moment did either of the two juniors think of the tattered lad they had rescued, weeks ago, from the brutality of Pedlar Parker. They had had only a passing glimpse of an unwashed face on that occasion. Some faint remembrance lingered, sufficient to give them a feeling that they had seen the boy before somewhere, but that was all. As for Dick, he had no recollection whatever of Wharton or his comrades, so far as looks went. He had scarcely glanced at them in that field near Compton Woods before he had fled to escape from the clutches of the pedlar.

"But very likely we've seen you before, if you've lived at Compton Hall," said Harry. "Might have passed you on the roads any time. Did you come over from the Hall to-day?"

"No; I've been in London with Sir Henry," said Dick. He did not say "my grandfather." Certainly Sir Henry was his grandfather by adoption, but somehow it seemed to ring untrue in his mind.

"What about tea?" asked Nugent. "We had a snack up the river, but I'm ready for tea – and I dare say Compton is, after his journey."

"Quite!" said Compton. "I've had some cake from your house-dame, but I'm ready for tea. Where do you have tea here?"

"In the study when the funds run to it," said Wharton, with a smile. "Of course, you can tea in Hall if you like. But we generally like it in the study if we can get it."

"Good!"

"You can cut down to the shop, Nugent, while I get a fire going," said the captain of the Remove.

"You buy the stuff yourselves?" asked Dick.

"Yes, at the school shop."

"Let me do your shopping, then. One of you fellows can show me the way."

"New kid bursting with tips from uncles and aunts!" chuckled Nugent.

"No, I haven't any uncles and aunts," said Dick. "But I've a lot of pocket-money."

"Hard cheese on poor old Bunter not to be here!" said Harry Wharton, laughing. "You're a chap Bunter would like to meet."

"Ha, ha, ha!"

"Who's Bunter?" asked Dick, little dreaming how well he had already made the acquaintance of that fat and fatuous youth.

"A Remove chap, the fattest fellow at Greyfriars, and a fellow who will borrow your last half-crown before you fairly know what he's doing," said the captain of the Remove. "Well, if you're well supplied you can go down to the shop with Nugent and put a few things on the list, and I'll ask three fellows to tea. You'd like to meet some Remove chaps — friends of ours?"

"Yes, rather!" said Dick brightly.

"Buzz off then!"

The new junior left the study with Frank Nugent; and Harry Wharton, after starting the fire, went along the passage to call Bob Cherry, Johnny Bull and Hurree Jamset Ram Singh to tea in Study No. 1.

"Tea with the new kid!" announced Wharton. "He's stuck in our study — but he seems a decent sort of chap. Quelchy says he's been in delicate health, but I'm blessed if he looks like it!'"

"The Remove isn't the place for a giddy invalid!" grunted Johnny Bull.

"He doesn't look much like an invalid now, if he ever was one. Come on — they'll be back with the grub!"

"Has Bunter made his acquaintance yet?" chuckled Bob Cherry. "It's a chance for his postal-order."

"Ha, ha! Bunter's not in yet! Smithy landed him at Lantham, and left him to walk home!"

"Ha, ha, ha! Poor old Bunter!"

The four juniors went along the Remove passage, and Peter Todd looked out of Study No. 7 as they passed.

"Seen anything of Bunter?" he asked. "He wasn't in to tea, and it's jolly near call-over now."

"Landed at Lantham, and walking home," answered Harry.

"What?"

Harry Wharton explained what he had heard from the Bounder. Peter Todd burst into a roar.

"Ha, ha, ha! Poor old Bunter! Ten to one he will try to bilk the railway company for a free ride!"

"Then he may get run in, and we mayn't see him any more!" chuckled Bob. "Let's hope for the best."

"Ha, ha, ha!"

Evidently there was a plentiful lack of sympathy for William George Bunter among his Form-fellows in the Remove. No doubt he deserved just as much as he received, and no more.

CHAPTER 17

Bunter in Luck!

BILLY BUNTER wore a worried look.

He had cause for worry.

The fat junior was seated in a taxicab, which had turned in at the gates of Greyfriars, and buzzed up the drive to the house.

Bunter was home again after his afternoon out. The problem of transport had been solved. He was back from Lantham. But it had been replaced by another problem; the still more perplexing problem of settling with the taxi-driver.

The meter indicated that William George Bunter owed the chauffeur the sum of seventeen shillings and ninepence when the taxi came to a halt. And William George Bunter's total financial resources consisted of one penny, which − being a bad one − had remained in his possession instead of following the usual route of Bunter's pocket-money to the tuck-shop. One penny, especially a bad one, was not much towards such a sum as seventeen shilling and ninepence. It was no wonder that a worried look had settled upon the Owl's fat visage.

Bunter had taken the taxi from Lantham because there was nothing else to be done. It had proved impracticable to "bilk" the railway company, and walking was out of the question for Bunter. The advantage of a taxi was that the

117

man had to be paid at the end of the journey instead of at the beginning like the railway. Bunter was, at all events, landed at Greyfriars in time for call-over, and that was the most important thing. But the end of the journey had now come, and Bunter knew that eloquence would be wasted on the taxi-driver. He would want seventeen shillings and nine-pence, and nothing less would satisfy him.

In the circumstances, considering how the playful Bounder had landed Bunter at Lantham that day, Smithy ought to stand the taxi fare, Bunter thought. He ought – it was certain that he ought – but Bunter doubted very much whether he would. In fact, he knew that he wouldn't. Peter Todd, as Bunter's study-mate, ought to shell out. But it was fairly certain that even if Peter had seventeen shillings and nine-pence at his disposal he would not part with it on Bunter's account.

If Mr. Quelch paid the man the bill would be sent in to Bunter's father, and that meant trouble twice over; first with Mr. Quelch and then with Mr. Bunter. That was a last desperate resource. Every other resource had to be tried first.

Bunter stepped out of the cab after a last blink at the meter. He blinked at the driver.

"Seventeen-and-nine on the clock, sir," said the man, evidently in expectation of something in addition for so long a drive.

That expectation did not worry Bunter. He did not mind disappointing anybody's expectations. But the seventeen-and-nine worried him deeply. Skinner was lounging on the steps, and he stared at Bunter and the taxi.

"Hallo, doing things in style, fatty?" he asked. "Have you come into a fortune?"

Bunter blinked round at Skinner.

"I say, Skinner, old chap, I've left my—my money in the study. Settle with this chap, will you, and I'll square later."

"Ha, ha, ha!" roared Skinner.

"What are you cackling at, you silly ass?" snapped Bunter. Billy Bunter, at least, was not in a mirthful mood.

"Your little joke!" chuckled Skinner.

"I'm not joking, you chump!"

"You are old man – you are! One of your best!" assured Skinner.

Evidently there was no assistance to be derived from Harold Skinner. Bunter turned his blink on the taxi-driver again.

"Hang on a minute or two," he said.

The man gave him a suspicious look.

"I'll hang on till I'm paid, sir; you rely on that," he said, with emphasis. "And the clock's going on, sir."

Bunter rolled into the house, leaving the taxi waiting. Somehow or other that man had to be paid. There was not the slightest doubt that he would wait till he had his money, if he had to wait all the evening and all night, for that matter. A low, grasping fellow, in Bunter's estimation. But there it was; he had to be paid.

Bunter blinked dismally in the direction of Mr. Quelch's study. But he simply dared not go to his Form-master with a confession that he had hired a taxi for a long journey and could not pay the fare. He limped upstairs to the Remove passage.

"Hallo, you've got back, old fat man!" It was Peter Todd's voice on the landing.

Bunter gave Peter an imploring blink.

"I–I say, Peter, I had to take a taxi from Lantham – "

"What?" roared Peter. "You've blued a quid on a taxi! Where did you get the quid?"

"The man isn't paid yet; he's waiting."

"Great Scott! He will be an experienced waiter by the time he gets his fare, I should say!"

"Lend me seventeen-and-nine!"

"Ha, ha, ha!" roared Peter.

Toddy, like Skinner, seemed to take the request as a

screaming joke. Bunter scowled at him and rolled on into Study No. 4. Tom Redwing and the Bounder were there, and they grinned at the sight of Bunter's woebegone face in the doorway.

"Crawled home – what?" asked the Bounder.

"I came in a taxi."

"Phew! That's rather expensive, isn't it?"

"The man's waiting to be paid."

"Ha, ha, ha!"

"Lend me a pound, Smithy," pleaded Bunter. "The man will kick up a row if he's not paid. You know what these common people are like about money. I shall get into a frightful row with Quelchy!"

"You will," agreed Smithy.

"Lend me – "

"Only my boot," said Vernon-Smith, jumping up. Bunter dodged out and slammed the door just in time to escape that undesired loan.

He groaned dismally, and made his way to Study No. 1. Harry Wharton was the last resource, and he had a deep and dismal foreboding that the captain of the Remove would be drawn blank. However, there was nothing to be lost by trying, and Bunter blinked into Study No. 1.

Three juniors were there. One of them sat with his back towards the door, but Bunter could see enough of him to observe that he was a newcomer. He guessed that this would be Compton, the new fellow he had missed, as he supposed – at Lantham that afternoon. His dismal face brightened just a little. Sir Henry Compton's grandson was bound to have money in his pockets. Borrowing from a fellow who did not know him might be a difficult task. But, really, it was easier for Bunter to borrow from a fellow who did not know him than from a fellow who did.

"I say, you fellows!"

"So you've got back from Lantham," said Harry Wharton,

laughing. "How did you get home? Bilk somebody? Or did you walk, Bunter?"

"Oh, really, Wharton — "

Ragged Dick started. He did not turn his head. He sat quite still, with a strange beating at his heart. He knew that fat voice. He remembered it very well. He knew that the fellow who had just come into the study was the fat fellow he had met at Lantham — the fellow who knew that he was Ragged Dick, the tattered tramp of a few weeks ago.

His face paled.

That fellow — that fat rascal — was a Greyfriars chap then. Bunter — Wharton had mentioned Bunter of the Remove! It was Bunter of the Remove he had met at Lantham — Bunter, who knew —

He sat quite still.

Billy Bunter's fat voice ran on:

"Of course, I couldn't walk that distance, Wharton. And a low beast of a porter found that I hadn't a ticket — I—I mean, of course, I wouldn't have travelled on the railway without a ticket. I hope I'm above that. I—I had to take a taxi."

"A taxi from Lantham!" exclaimed Nugent. "Why, that must be fifteen bob, at least?"

"Seventeen-and-nine," said Bunter. "Eighteen by this time, or more. The beast is keeping his meter ticking! I say, you fellows, lend me a quid!"

"I can see us doing it!" remarked Nugent.

"You silly owl!" exclaimed Harry Wharton, staring at the fat junior. "Do you think fellows have quids to throw away on taxi fares! You'd better go to Quelch."

"It means a frightful row!" groaned Bunter. "I—I say, you fellows, you know I'm expecting a postal-order — "

"Ha, ha, ha!"

"Beasts!"

As Bunter had dismally anticipated, the captain of the

Remove was drawn blank. But the new fellow was there, and he was Bunter's last hope — and the faintest chance had to be tried before Mr. Quelch was approached on the subject.

"I suppose that's Compton," said Bunter, blinking at the back of the new junior's head, wondering a little why the fellow did not take the trouble to glance round.

"That's Compton, this is Bunter, the fat bounder I mentioned to you. If you lend him any money, you'll never see it again. That's a tip."

"You mind your own business!" roared Bunter indignantly. "I suppose Compton can lend me a pound if he likes!"

"Certainly — if he's ass enough!"

"I say, Compton — "

Dick did not move.

He seemed frozen to his chair. Who could have foreseen this? Certainly Sir Henry Compton, in bringing Ragged Dick to Greyfriars as his grandson, had never foreseen anything of the kind happening. He was known! This fat fellow knew him; knew that he was Ragged Dick, knew that he was an imposter — for that was what it would be called. In a few minutes Wharton and Nugent would know — in an hour all Greyfriars! What could he say! Could he deny it — pile falsehood on falsehood? He knew that he could not.

This was the end — the sudden end of the happy school life he had dreamed of. He sat overwhelmed.

"I say, Compton," repeated Bunter. As the new junior did not stir, Bunter rolled farther into the study and came round in front of him. "I say, old chap, you'll do a fellow a good turn, won't you? I'm expecting a postal-order by the first post in the morning, but I happen to be short of a quid. I—why—what—what—what— "

Bunter broke off, stuttering.

He stared at the new junior's handsome pale face — stared at it as if it had been the face of a spectre. He was so astonished that his fat jaw dropped. He stared and stared, scarcely able to believe his eyes or his spectacles.

Dick looked steadily at him.

The blow was falling. He had to summon his courage to meet it. He did not expect Bunter to be silent. Why should he?

"You!" stuttered Bunter at last.

"Hallo, have you seen Compton before, too? asked Harry Wharton.

Bunter gave a gasping chuckle.

"That's Compton, is it?"

"That's Compton," said Nugent. "Half a dozen chaps think they've seen him before somewhere. Are you another?"

"Great Scott!"

Bunter grinned.

"I fancy I've seen him before. I met him this afternoon at Lantham, didn't I, Compton? He, he, he!"

"Yes!" breathed Dick.

"You met Bunter!" exclaimed Harry in surprise. "You didn't mention – "

"I did not know his name," said Dick in a low, husky voice. "I didn't know he belonged to Greyfriars."

"I see."

"And I didn't know you belonged to Greyfriars!" chortled Bunter. "Not the least bit! My only hat! It's like your cheek to come here!"

"What do you mean, Bunter?" asked Wharton testily. "Why shouldn't Compton come here, you fat ass?"

"He, he, he!"

Dick waited in silence. It was all coming out now. But it did not come! Bunter was amazed, puzzled, perplexed. He didn't know how to make head or tail of this strange affair. But one thing was quite clear to Bunter's fat mind, and that was that this fellow, Ragged Dick, or Richard Compton, or whoever or whatever he was, was under his fat thumb.

Bunter's podgy brain did not, as a rule, work very quickly; but it could work quickly enough when he had a turn to serve, as undoubtedly he had.

He grinned cheerily.

"Well, here he is," he said. "I met him at Lantham. He, he, he! Do you know, I was going to borrow my railway fare off him, and he refused. He, he, he! Mean, you know! But I feel sure he will oblige me by settling with that taximan – won't you, Compton? He, he, he!"

Dick looked at him hard. There was no mistaking the mocking grin on Bunter's fat face. His silence was to be had – if it was paid for! Dick understood.

"What rot!" exclaimed Wharton. "Don't let that fat bounder diddle you out of a pound, Compton! You'll never see it again!"

Dick rose to his feet.

"You're going to settle that little matter for me, old chap, what?" grinned Bunter.

"Yes."

"Give him a quid, old man. After all, he ought to have a tip after driving me from Lantham!" Bunter could be generous where his own money was not concerned.

"Very well."

Dick left the study.

Billy Bunter turned a triumphant blink on Wharton and Nugent.

"It's all serene, you see," he chuckled.

"Compton must be an ass!" said Nugent.

"He, he, he!"

"After all, Bunter generally does diddle a new chap," said Wharton, with a shrug of the shoulders. "Compton will soon come to know him as well as we do."

"He, he, he!"

"Oh, get out, you fat bounder!"

Billy Bunter rolled out of Study No. 1 with a fat chuckle.

He was feeling extremely satisfied. His satisfaction was not shared by Ragged Dick of the Remove.

He paid off the taxi, and was returning along the Remove passage when he ran into Billy Bunter. The Owl of the Remove gave him a knowing wink, which brought the colour to Compton's cheeks.

"Come into the study, old chap," smiled Bunter.

And Compton, compressing his lips hard, followed William George Bunter into Study No. 7.

CHAPTER 18

What Bunter Knew!

"RAGGED DICK – "

Bunter grinned as he uttered that name.

Compton looked at him. The expression on his face made Bunter back away a little, and place the study table between him and the new Removite.

"Don't get waxy, old man," said the Owl of the Remove soothingly. "We're friends, ain't we?"

"Friends?" said Dick, with a contemptuous curl of the lip.

"I'm no snob," said Bunter cheerily. "I know what you are, and I'm prepared to be friendly, if you do the decent thing, of course."

"You fat rotter!"

"Oh, really, Compton – "

"What do you want?" snapped the new junior. "Look here, Bunter, this has got to stop. Already the fellows are suspicious at my lending you money."

"Oh, really, you rotter. I shall settle, of course, when – when I get my postal-order."

"Oh, cut out that rot! I know your sort."

"Look here!" roared Bunter.

"I'm fed-up with it, and with you," said Dick savagely. "You don't seem to understand what a disgraceful fat blackguard you are. But it's got to stop, see?"

Bunter's eyes gleamed behind his spectacles.

The Owl of the Remove was not thin-skinned. But it is said that contempt will pierce the shell of the tortoise; and even Bunter was not quite so thick-skinned as that.

"Why, you cheeky cad!" he exclaimed indignantly. "And what are you, I'd like to know, coming here as the grandson of Sir Henry Compton, and all the time you're a tattered tramp. Think I've forgotten the time when I met you in Compton Park – ragged and dirty, and hungry – and you told me your name was Ragged Dick –what a name! He, he, he! Then you turn up here calling yourself Richard Compton! I wonder what the Head would say?"

Dick breathed hard.

He, too, wondered what the Head would say if he knew.

Wrath gathered in the Owl's fat face. His very spectacles gleamed with it as he blinked at the new junior.

"What would the Head say?" he repeated. "Like me to go to the Head or Mr. Quelch and tell them all about you, you dashed impostor?"

Dick winced.

Was he an imposter? He hardly knew. But the word had a bitter sound to his ears, deserved or not.

"What were you like when I saw you in Compton Park that day?" pursued Bunter. "Dirty, in rags and tatters! Hungry and dirty – a rank outsider! Yah! Then you turn up here well-dressed, with lots of money in your pockets! There's a swindle somewhere."

And Bunter wagged his bullet head sagaciously.

He was certain there was a swindle somewhere. What sort of a swindle he could not even guess; but there it was! A lot about Dick Compton wanted explaining.

"Sir Henry Compton brought me here!" Dick said quietly. "You know that."

Bunter nodded.

"I know!" he answered. "That's what beats me! You seem

127

to be his grandson or he thinks you are. But if you are, how was it you were in rags and tatters sneaking about the woods, only a few weeks before you came to Greyfriars? That's what I want to know."

"Is it any business of yours?" snapped Compton.

"Perhaps it isn't, and perhaps it is!" sneered Bunter. "If you're an imposter – and it looks like it – it's a fellow's duty to show you up."

"Why don't you, then?"

Bunter was a little taken aback.

"Well, I don't want to be hard on a chap," he said. "I suppose old Compton knows his own business, and he's your grandfather, or says he is. But there's something fishy about it – some sort of swindle."

Dick crimsoned.

"There's no swindle," he said. "But if you think there is, Bunter, it's your duty to go straight to the headmaster and tell him."

"Do you want me to?" sneered Bunter.

"You can do as you choose," said Compton contemptuously. "You think you're going to get money out of me to keep your rascally mouth shut. That's got to stop!"

"You cheeky cad!" gasped Bunter, in great indignation. "Nothing of the kind! One good turn deserves another. Do you thing a fellow's going to keep your shady secrets if you don't treat him decently?"

"No fellow has a right to keep a shady secret," said Ragged Dick. "If you think it's shady, don't keep it."

"Isn't it shady?" howled Bunter.

"No."

"All fair and above-board – a tattered tramp turning up here as a baronet's grandson?" sneered Bunter. "It's too thick. If it's not shady, why can't you tell a chap how it came about?"

"I don't choose."

"Oh, come off!" said the Owl of the Remove derisively. "You've practically owned up it's shady. You were fairly scared out of your wits when I saw you in Wharton's study. Ragged Dick in the Greyfriars Remove! You wouldn't be in the Remove long if the Head knew all about you!"

"Tell him, then!" said Dick savagely.

He turned to the door.

"I say — "

Compton left the study and went down the stairs. His face was angry and determined. He was done with Bunter, whatever might come of it. Better for the facts to become known. whatsoever the results might be, than to live under the Owl's fat thumb.

Yet, for all that passionate resolve, Ragged Dick found himself wavering when next he encountered William George Bunter, and he decided to pay the fat junior for his silence until he should receive a reply to a letter he had hurriedly written to Sir Henry Compton. Which was all to the good where Billy Bunter was concerned, for it meant unlimited tuck for the next few days.

Still, even Bunter began to realise that the horn of plenty was running dry, whereupon he made no bones about informing Ragged Dick that he now "considered it his duty to tell the Remove" the shady secret of the boy who passed among them as Sir Henry's grandson and heir.

"Get on with it and be blowed! You'll never get another penny out of me, you fat rotter!" Ragged Dick had reached the limit of his patience and endurance, and the letter he had just received from Sir Henry had not improved his temper. "And now get out before I kick you out!"

"Yah!" roared Bunter defiantly. "You're a swindler, and I'm blessed if I'll keep your shady secret any longer. I'm going to tell the fellows now!"

Compton made a threatening move towards him, and the fat Owl of the Remove scuttled away as if for dear life.

Undoubtedly the horn of plenty had run dry!

With a moody brow Compton picked up his cap and walked out of gates. He wanted to be alone to think – to read once again the short, curt reply he had received from Sir Henry Compton.

CHAPTER 19

In Dark Doubt!

" **I**T'S 'im! "
   The dirty, shabby, ill-favoured man lounging in the shade of the leafy trees in Friardale Lane muttered the words, with a glint in his bleary eyes.

Pedlar Parker had spotted his prey at last.

Day after day Pedlar Parker had hung about the precincts of Greyfriars School; a good many of the Greyfriars fellows had noticed him at different times. Indeed, Coker of the Fifth had helped him on his way with a boot, finding him loafing about the school gates. But there was some attraction for the ruffian in the precincts of the old school, and day after day he might have been seen lurking about the roads and lanes, or sprawling under the hedges, dirty, tattered, surly and determined. And now he had found what he sought.

A junior was coming down the lane, and Pedlar Parker's glinting eyes fixed on him as he lounged under the trees.

It was Compton of the Remove — Ragged Dick of former days.

The new junior certainly looked very handsome and fit. A very startling change from the Ragged Dick Mr. Parker had known. But he was the same fellow — Pedlar Parker was quite convinced of that.

Dick's brow was slightly clouded, and his eyes were on the

ground in deep thought. He was not looking about him, and he did not see the pedlar in the shade of the old beeches and oaks.

"It's 'im!" repeated Pedlar Parker, with an oath.

There was hatred in the stare he fixed on the unconscious junior of Greyfriars.

Dick's evident prosperity, his rise in fortune, embittered the tattered ruffian who had once been his tyrant. Idleness and loafing and petty thieving had not enriched Mr. Parker; there were, indeed, more kicks than halfpence to be gathered up in his career as a snatcher-up of unconsidered trifles. That the boy whom he had known ragged and forlorn was now well-dressed, healthy and happy did not please Mr. Parker — the milk of human kindness had been left out of his composition. He was thinking of sharing, somehow, in Ragged Dick's fortune: but he would almost rather have destroyed it than shared in it.

Ragged Dick stopped, only for a dozen yards from the lurking tramp, and drew a letter from his pocket. He leaned against a tree by the side of the lane and re-read the letter with a clouded brow, unconscious of the savage eyes watching him.

"Compton Hall" Kent

"Dear Richard, — I received your letter. Kindly do not write on the same topic again. I expect unquestioning obedience from my grandson."

"HENRY COMPTON."

Dick knew the letter by heart now. It troubled him.

He had written to the old baronet from Greyfriars. What he had not dared to ask the stern old man by word of mouth he had ventured to put into writing.

Timidly, respectfully, he pointed out the position, and asked, since Sir Henry had been so kind and generous as to adopt him, whether he could not add to his kindness by letting the adoption be known.

It seemed to Dick that there was no objection to be urged against such a step. It was impossible – for Dick, at least – to suppose that Sir Henry had any questionable motive for what he had done.

He did not seem a kind man, yet what motive could he have but kindness?

Once the facts were known at Greyfriars the burden would be off the boy's mind. He did not care much if the fellows knew his origin. He had already learned that most of the Greyfriars fellows – all the best of them, at least – valued a chap for what he was, and what he could do, rather than for what his ancestors had been or had done. Snobbish fellows like Skinner and Snoop, or Angel of the Fourth, might turn up their noses at Ragged Dick. He would not care for that, so long as Harry Wharton & Co. liked Ragged Dick as much as they liked Richard Compton. Indeed, he did not want to gain any fellow's friendship on false pretences.

And this was the baronet's reply!

Evidently he would not hear of it. Unquestioning obedience; he was entitled to that. He was entitled to the loyal devotion, unremitting and life-long, of the boy he had saved from rags and want. But – if only he would have let him tell the truth!

Dick sighed.

There was nothing to be hoped for from the old baronet, that was clear. For reasons Dick could not even guess at he was determined to keep on as he had begun. He must have some reasons. Little did poor Dick dream of suspecting what the reasons were – that the entailed estates and the title of Compton could only descend to an heir by blood, and not to an heir by adoption. The baronet's reasons were powerful ones, but Ragged Dick did not dream of suspecting them. He was not likely to suspect that he was an unconscious party to a fraud practised on the heir-in-entail to the Compton title and estates.

But would not Sir Henry's hand be forced if Bunter told what he knew?

Bunter's story, true as it was, seemed a wild one, and might very likely be laughed at at Greyfriars. It would probably be taken as another of Bunter's yarns. But Dick would have to deny it. And he could not deny it without steeping himself in falsehood.

Would Sir Henry expect that of him? Could he render unquestioning obedience to that extent?

It came into Dick's mind that, in some respects at least, he had been more carefree in his old days tramping the roads.

He crushed the letter in his hand at last. It was time to get back to the school for tea, and yet he hesitated to go back. If Bunter had betrayed him, and told the story of Ragged Dick, he would have a curious crowd to face – fellows who probably would not believe a word that Bunter had said, yet would probably ask him about it. Deny the story – piling lie on lie in the manner of Bunter himself – he revolted at the thought. Admit it – breaking his promise to Sir Henry – disobeying his strict commands! The only alternative was silence, and how would the silence be construed?

Plunged in grim and gloomy reflection, Ragged Dick did not observe the ill-favoured, slinking figure that was creeping towards him till Pedlar Parker's shadow fell across his face.

He started and looked up.

His hands clenched convulsively, his eyes dilated, the colour fled from his cheeks, as he stared blankly at the evil face before him.

"You!" he breathed.

CHAPTER 20

Ragged Dick's Defiance!

PEDLAR PARKER chuckled.

His eyes gleamed evilly as they were fixed on the startled face of the schoolboy of Greyfriars.

He had been assured, convinced, that this well-dressed fellow was in reality Ragged Dick, the tattered companion of his tramping. Yet at the back of his evil mind a doubt lingered. The change in the boy's fortune was so amazing, so astounding, that Parker had been haunted by a doubt that it might turn out to be only some case of a strange resemblance.

Had Compton of the Remove given him an indifferent glance, the glance of a fellow who had never seen him before. Pedlar Parker would have been baffled; he would have been driven to the conclusion that this well-dressed schoolboy was, after all, only a fellow who by some strange chance closely resembled the boy who had escaped from him.

But Dick was not on his guard; the sudden sight of the ruffian had taken him quite by surprise, and it did not even occur to his mind to play a part.

His dismayed stare, his startled ejaculation, were the proof that the ruffian wanted. It was Ragged Dick who stood before him.

"You!" repeated Dick blankly.

"Me!" chuckled the pedlar hoarsely. "Your old pal, Parker.

Glad to see me, ain't you, Dick?"

Dick shrank back from the ruffian's face, the foul breath, tainted with spirits.

"Let me alone!" he muttered.

" 'Ardly believed it was you, though I knowed it was all the time," chuckled Parker. "We're a toff these 'ere days, ain't we – a blooming toff! Ain't got 'ardly a word for an old pal!"

Dick pulled himself together.

"You never were a pal of mine, you rotter! You were a thieving rascal, and I never wanted to tramp with you, and you know it. I got away from you as soon as I could. Now I don't want anything to say to you. Clear off!"

Pedlar Parker grinned evilly.

"You don't want nothing to say to me now you're up in the stirrups?" he jeered. "How did you come by your fine clothes? What are you doing in the school, eh?"

"No business of yours."

"Couldn't believe me eyes when I saw you with the old gent in the taxi going into Greyfriars School!" said Parker. "I knowed there was some game on. How did you get round the old gent?"

Dick did not answer.

He was startled and dismayed by the meeting, but he quickly recovered his nerve. He was not afraid of Pedlar Parker; the days were over when he had been a forlorn waif and the ruffian had forced him to tramp in his company. He understood how amazed the ruffian must be at having seen him in company with Sir Henry Compton; in seeing him a well-dressed Greyfriars fellow, and it was natural that Parker should suspect that the change had come about by some trickery or other. But certainly he had no intention of explaining to the ruffian.

He stood silent, his hands clenching hard. He was no match for the ruffian physically, but he was prepared to give as good an account of himself as possible if Parker proceeded to violence.

"How did you work it?" asked Parker, with evident curiosity. "You fooled that old gent somehow. What?"

No answer.

"I've found out the name of that there school. It's Greyfriars. Do you belong to Greyfriars School?"

"Yes."

"And you ain't got even a name? What do they call you there?"

"Find out!"

"I'm going to," said Pedlar Parker, with bitter emphasis. "I'm going to 'ave a 'and in this game, young Dick. I'm going to 'ave a share. You've got money in your pockets these days; You've got good clothes on your back. You was pretty ragged and dirty when you was with me, and I used to lay into you with my stick."

"Yes, you brute!" said Dick between his teeth. "I've good clothes and money in my pockets; and not a sixpence to give you. Get on your way, you hound, and leave me to get on mine!"

The pedlar's eyes glinted.

"That's the language, is it, now?" he sneered. "High and mighty in our noo clothes! I want to know the name you're goin' by at Greyfriars School."

"Find out, you rotter!"

"Who was that old gent I saw you with in the taxi?"

"Find out that, too?"

"I s'pose he's the bloke what sent you to the school, eh?"

"You can keep on asking questions, but I shan't answer any," replied Ragged Dick, with cool contempt.

"Well, it's pretty clear," said Pedlar Parker. "That's 'ow I've worked it out. Somehow you got round that old feller, and he's fixed you up like this and sent you to school. You always was one for learning, I remember. P'r'aps some sort of a yarn about that did the trick – what? Though that old bloke didn't look soft, either."

Dick smile involuntarily.

Pedlar Parker, in his surmises as to how Ragged Dick had "worked" that change in his fortunes, was never likely to hit on anything near the truth. Certainly his surmise that Sir Henry Compton had been imposed upon by a beggar's tale was wide of the mark. The grim old baronet, as Parker himself had recognised, was an extremely unlikely man to be imposed upon. Yet there it was; it was fairly clear that the man he had seen Dick with in the taxi had taken up the waif and sent him to school. Why?

"You won't let a bloke into the game – what?" asked Parker, eyeing the Greyfriars junior savagely.

"There isn't any game on, as you call it."

"Mean to say that that old ramrod of a cove took you up out of pure kindness of 'eart?" jeered the pedlar.

"I mean to say nothing to you!" answered Dick coolly.

"You've pulled his leg somehow," said Parker. "You've spun him some yarn that he's taken in. He don't look that sort, but that must be it, 'cause why, there ain't any other reason why he should spend money on you like this. Well, if you're taking him in, and pulling his leg on your own account, Ragged Dick, you can put on an extra turn of the screw for me. See?"

Dick shrugged his shoulders.

"I'm in this," said Parker. "You catch on – right in it! Halves, my covey."

"Are you finished?" said Dick.

"Halves, I tell you. How much 'ave you got about you now?"

"Three or four pounds."

"Two for me, then; and more to foller," said Pedlar Parker, holding out a dirty hand.

"I will not give you a sixpence."

"P'r'aps you'd rather I came into the school and told the young gents about you?" sneered Parker.

"Come into the school – if you dare!" retorted Dick. "I fancy you wouldn't get past the porter. You'd be kicked out if you did."

The pedlar gritted his teeth. As a matter of fact, he knew that Ragged Dick was right on that point.

"Mean to say the 'eadmaster of that big school knows about you?" he asked, after a savage pause. "Knows you was a tramp on the road afore that old covey put you to school?"

Dick did not answer.

Parker was perplexed and puzzled; and Dick had no intention whatever of helping him out of his perplexity.

"You ain't telling me anything?" asked Parker.

"Nothing."

"You won't tell me 'ow you got round the old covey?"

"Nothing at all."

"And you won't share out with an old pal?"

"I will give you nothing – nothing at all! Threaten me as much as you like, you'll get nothing out of me," answered Dick steadily.

"And s'pose," hissed the enraged ruffian, "suppose I take you by the neck and hide you, like I used to when we was tramping together."

"I'll give you back all I can," said Dick quietly, "and you'll find me a bit tougher than you found me then, Parker. I'm not half-starved now, nor tired with tramping in all weathers. I fancy I could give you a tussle, Pedlar Parker. I'll try, anyhow, and if you lay a finger on me I'll put the police after you, too, like any other Greyfriars chap would."

Parker trembled with rage.

"You a Greyfriars chap! You put the police on me!" he said, in a choking voice.

"Certainly! Any decent fellow attacked by a tramp would inform the police, and have the rotter put in prison," said

Dick. "And that's exactly what I shall do, Pedlar Parker; and you know best whether you want trouble with the police or not. You generally had stolen goods about you, or in your pack, when I knew you, and I've no doubt it's the same now. Better let me alone."

Pedlar Parker eyed him, shaking with fury. He realised the truth that was in the Greyfriars junior's words; the power was in Dick's hands now to obtain adequate protection against any ruffianly tramp on the road. He was no longer the forlorn and friendless waif whom the brutal outcast had ill-used. And Parker most assuredly did not want to come into personal contact with the police. His feud with the gentlemen in blue was an ancient one; the mere sight of the uniform of a guardian of the law was generally enough to make Mr. Parker slink out of his road.

But in his rage at the defiance of this boy, whom he had once beaten without mercy, Pedlar Parker forgot all prudence. That the boy, whether by trickery or not, had a powerful protector in the stern old gentleman Parker had seen him with – that, by trickery or not, he was now a member of a big school whose headmaster would certainly take the matter up if he were assaulted by a tramp. Parker realised all this, but, in his fury, he threw aside all considerations of his own safety. He was not to share in the new fortunes of Ragged Dick. It was doubtful whether he could even injure him by betraying him, and his hatred swelled almost to madness. With glinting eyes, snarling almost like a wild animal, the ruffian fairly hurled himself at the Greyfriars junior.

Dick was watching him keenly, ready for the attack. He leaped back as it came, actively, and then sprang aside. Before the enraged ruffian could turn upon him he struck out with all the force of his sinewy young arm.

Crash!

There was a hoarse grunt of pain from Pedlar Parker as he caught the clenched fist on the side of his jaw.

He went with a crash into the grass.

Dick leaped out into the lane to run for it. But the pedlar, sprawling in the grass, clutched at him as he leaped and caught his ankle. Dick came down in the road heavily.

"My turn now!" panted the ruffian.

He scrambled into the road after the fallen junior, still gripping him. Dick turned on him, and they struggled, the junior hitting out fiercely; while the ruffian, scarcely conscious in his rage of the blows he received, rained savage blows on Ragged Dick.

CHAPTER 21

Handling a Hooligan!

"**S**TOP that!"

"Great Scott!"

Two seniors of Greyfriars were strolling up the lane from Friardale towards the school when they came in sight of that startling scene. Wingate, the captain of Greyfriars, and Gwynne, of the Sixth, were chatting football as they sauntered along in the pleasant afternoon, at peace with themselves and all the world.

But the sight of a junior in Etons struggling frantically in the grasp of a hulking tramp, who was raining blows on him, startled the two Sixth Formers out of their cheery equanimity. Wingate broke into a rapid run, shouting as he ran up, and Gwynne was hardly a moment behind him.

"Help!" panted Dick, as he heard Wingate's voice.

"Stop that!" roared Wingate.

His grasp was on the pedlar the next moment.

Pedlar Parker was a burly ruffian, but the athletic captain of Greyfriars whirled him off his victim with ease. The pedlar went crashing into the grass by the road.

He sprawled there, breathless, panting out curses. Ragged Dick sat up rather dazedly in the dust.

"It's a Greyfriars kid," said Gwynne, staring down at Dick. "That new kid in the Remove, I think — "

142

"Compton!" said Wingate. "Are you hurt, Compton?" He gave the gasping junior a hand up.

Dick panted for breath.

"Only a little. It's all right."

"Was that brute trying to rob you?" asked Wingate. "My hat! Almost within sight of the school gates!"

He turned towards Pedlar Parker, who had sat up in the grass and was eyeing him savagely.

"Get up, you hound!" said Wingate.

"Burn you!" hissed Parker. "I — "

"Get up! Had he taken anything from you, Compton?"

"No!" gasped Dick.

"That was his game, of course," said Gwynne. "And he would have scored if we hadn't come up."

Wingate nodded.

"The brute's going to have a lesson," he said.

He fixed his eyes on the tramp.

"Get up! I won't take the trouble to kick you as far as the village and hand you over to the police! I'm going to thrash you! Get up!"

Pedlar Parker scrambled savagely to his feet.

"I ain't done any 'arm!" he panted. "I've a right to wallop that there kid if I choose. He belongs to me!"

Wingate, who was taking off his coat, paused to stare at the man, amazed.

"Are you mad or drunk?" he asked.

"I ain't neither," hissed Parker savagely. "If you belong to that school yonder, and I s'pose you do, you know who that kid is."

"Certainly I know," answered Wingate. "He is a Greyfriars boy, and I am going to thrash you for interfering with him!"

"And what's he called at Greyfriars?"

"No business of yours!"

"I tell you that kid belongs to me!" said Pedlar Parker, with husky fury. "He was my mate tramping the roads till he run away one day."

"The fellow's mad!" said Gwynne, in wonder.

"I can tell you his name!" hissed the pedlar. "He's Dick, he is — Ragged Dick. He ain't got any other name!"

Ragged Dick, leaning against a tree, panting for breath, felt his heart almost stop beating. It was coming out now.

But the pedlar's statement only caused Gwynne of the Sixth to stare at him with amused surprise, while Wingate gave a grunt of contempt.

The Greyfriars captain threw his coat to Gwynne, and pushed back his cuffs. He was in deadly earnest, Wingate was a good-natured fellow, but the sight of the ruffian raining blows on a struggling boy had stirred his deepest ire. He was going to give Pedlar Parker some of his own medicine; which, in his opinion, was exactly what the scoundrel wanted.

"I tell you it's the truth!" hissed Parker. "That kid was a tramp on the road only a few weeks ago, and he was called Ragged Dick, and he never had a name. If you belong to his school you know it's so."

"Drunk, I suppose," said Gwynne, in wonder, "or else potty! Do you think you will make anyone believe that a baronet's grandson was tramping the road with you at any time, you silly ruffian?"

Parker stared.

"A—a baronet's grandson!" he stuttered. "Him! Oh, that's too rich! Oh, my eye!"

"Are you ready, you scoundrel?" asked Wingate grimly.

"You keep your 'ands off a bloke!" said Pedlar Parker. "I ain't got any quarrel with you. That kid's Ragged Dick, and he owned up to it jest afore you come up. I swear — "

"Oh, don't be a fool!" snapped Wingate. "The kid's name is Compton, and his grandfather is Sir Henry Compton, of Compton Hall. If you've mistaken him for somebody else, that's your look-out. I'm going to thrash you for attacking him, so put up your hands!"

"I tell you – " hisssed Parker.

But the ruffian had no time to tell more, if he had more to tell. Wingate was advancing on him, hitting out, and Pedlar Parker had to put up his grimy hands in self-defence.

"Go it, old bean!" grinned Gwynne.

Wingate was "going it." Parker defended himself with savage fury; but the champion athlete of Greyfriars was rather too much for him. There was a crash as the pedlar went down on his back in the dust.

"Man down!" chuckled Gwynne.

The ruffian sprawled in the road, a torrent of foul words streaming from his lips. Wingate glanced at Dick.

"Cut off, kid!" he said sharply.

"Yes, Wingate!"

Ragged Dick hurried off towards the school, glad to get off the scene. Parker struggled to his feet as Dick disappeared up the road.

"I'm going after that kid!" he said. "He's a swindling young hound, he is, and he's taken the old gent in somehow. I'm going to have him on the road again, and I'll hide him – by gum, I'll hide him till his skin comes off under my belt! I'll – "

"Put up your hands, you foul-mouthed brute!" rapped out Wingate.

And the pedlar had to dismiss Ragged Dick from his mind as the captain of Greyfriars came at him with a left and right.

For some minutes there was a terrific fight.

The ruffian fought his hardest, with the fury of a wild-cat, and Wingate for a little while had his hands full. The rugged face of the captain of Greyfriars showed a good many marks.

But he was getting the upper hand, slowly but steadily, and at length the pedlar went into the grass again, breathless, spent, bruised, and thrashed, beaten to the wide.

He lay there, panting, regarding Wingate with half-closed eyes that gleamed with hatred and malice.

The captain of Greyfriars looked on him grimly.

"Have you had enough, you brute?"

"Yes!" breathed Parker.

"I'll let you off with that, then. But get out of this neigh-bourhood," said Wingate. "You could be put in prison, and you know it, for attacking young Compton; and if I find you hanging about here again, I'll see that it's done, too. Better tramp while you've got the chance."

Wingate put on his coat, and walked away towards the school with Gwynne of the Sixth.

The two Sixth Formers disappeared from the ruffian's view, as he lay gasping and groaning by the road.

He lay there a long time, too spent to stir. Seldom or never, in all his lawless career, had Pedlar Parker received so terrific a thrashing, though doubtless he had often deserved it.

He was thinking, savagely, evilly, as he lay and groaned. There was nothing to be got from the one-time waif. How-ever Ragged Dick had come by his good fortune, there was no share in it for his former tyrant. The ruffian had thought of seizing him by force, and dragging him back to the tramp-ing life of the road; but he realised that it was out of his power. Grandson of a baronet – grandson of Sir Henry Compton, of Compton Park! How had Ragged Dick done it – how had he imposed on that severe-looking old gentle-man whom the pedlar had seen taking him into the school a week ago? If the old man had placed him at school as his grandson, he must believe that the boy was his grandson – somehow, by unimaginable trickery, Ragged Dick had imposed upon him. But how, how? For it could not be true. Ragged Dick could not be the man's grandson!

The ruffian rose at last, groaning. A glimmer of white in the grass caught his eye. He had been lying on a letter, which had fallen in the grass, undoubtedly from Ragged Dick's hand when the ruffian had attacked him. Parker remembered that the boy had been reading a letter.

He picked it up and looked at it. It was the letter from Sir Henry Compton to his grandson in the Greyfriars Remove.

"My eye!" murmured Parker.

It was true, then, what those two contemptuous fellows had said — the boy was supposed to be a baronet's grandson. No wonder they had heard his statements with derision. Yet he had told the truth. Ragged Dick was Ragged Dick, a tramp of the roads; he was not, and could not be, grandson to Sir Henry Compton, of Compton Hall.

Pedlar Parker put the letter into his pocket, and loafed away, still mumbling over his injuries. It seemed that he could not harm Ragged Dick at his school. His story, told there, would be laughed at, treated with derision as Wingate and Gwynne had treated it. But there was another resource. Somehow, by some amazing deceit, as it seemed indubitably to Parker, Ragged Dick had imposed himself upon an old man; somehow, Sir Henry Compton had been made to believe that the tattered waif was his grandson. There, at least, the rascal could intervene; to the old baronet, at least, he could expose the cheat — he could tell him who and what Ragged Dick really was. There might be a reward to come for opening the old man's eyes to the deception. At least it would spoil Ragged Dick's game — queer his pitch, as the ruffian expressed it in his evil thoughts.

And the pedlar tramped away, his mind made up, deriving what consolation he could from the thought of "queering the pitch" for Ragged Dick with Sir Henry Compton, of Compton Hall.

CHAPTER 22

"Chuck it, Bunter!"

"I SAY, you fellows – "
Billy Bunter had wasted no time. The moment he realised that Compton meant what he said, the fat junior rolled into the Rag in search of an audience to listen to his amazing story.

That it was possible his strange story would never be believed, that it would be put down as a stupid fabrication in Bunter's customary style, the fat junior never considered for one moment.

"I say, you fellows – " he began, as he burst into the Rag, where Skinner & Co., Tom Brown and Squiff, and Bolsover Major were chatting, "that young rotter Compton is a fraud."

Skinner & Co. looked up. Like the rest of the Removites, they had noticed that Billy Bunter seemed to possess some "hold" over the new boy, as for the past few days the Owl of the Remove had been rolling in funds. He made no secret of it, either, that his "pal" Compton had cashed one or two postal orders in advance.

"Won't he cash any more postal orders for you, old fat man?" inquired Bolsover major shrewdly. "looks to me as if he's found out that you're the fraud."

"Oh, really, Bolsover. I tell you the fellow's a fraud – an imposter. He's a tramp."

"Eh?"

"What?"

"Which?"

Even Tom Brown and Squiff were interested now. They gathered round the fat junior curiously.

Billy Bunter had succeeded in astonishing the Removites.

"Who's a tramp?"

"That fellow Compton," said Bunter eagerly. "I'm going to give him away – I'm not going to keep his shady secrets for him. His name's not Compton at all really – he's called Ragged Dick."

"Is the fat idiot mad?" asked Skinner, staring blankly at the Owl of the Remove.

"Must be, I think?" said Bolsover.

"Compton's the grandson of old Sir Henry Compton at Compton Hall," said Snoop. "What do you mean by saying that his name's not Compton, Bunter?"

"It isn't, all the same. I saw him before he came to Greyfriars, and he was a ragged tramp and a beggar – "

"Sir Henry Compton's grandson was?" howled Skinner.

"Yes. I saw him, and – "

"Well, I've heard some pretty steep yarns from Bunter before," said Skinner. "But I think this one takes the cake. You fat dummy, do you think we're going to believe a silly yarn like that about Compton, when we know you've only made it up because he won't lend you any more money?"

Bunter started.

It had not occurred to his fat mind that that view might be taken of his startling story.

"I've not made it up!" he exclaimed. "I tell you I met the fellow in Compton Park, before he came to Greyfriars, and he was dirty and in rags and tatters."

"Yes, Sir Henry would be likely to let his grandson go around his park in rags and tatters – I don't think!"

"He wasn't his grandson – he told me he was a tramp,

tramping the roads, without a home — "

"If he had told you anything of the sort, you fat idiot, he was pulling your leg," said Skinner. "Not that I believe a word of it! It's too jolly clear why you're spinning a yarn about Compton! You've been sticking him for loans, and he's chucked it up!"

"Oh, really, Skinner — "

"If you want to spin a yarn about a chap, why don't you make it a bit more probable?" grinned Skinner. "Tell us that he pinched his grandfather's gold watch and popped it with Lazarus, in Courtfield. Tell us that he goes to the races, blagging, with that precious Roger Compton we've heard about, and comes home squiffy at one in the morning. Tell us anything — except that fatheaded yarn you've just told us."

"Yes, make it a bit more probable, Bunter," chuckled Snoop. "Begin again at the beginning, and not so steep this time."

"You silly asses!" howled Bunter. "It's true. I tell you that fellow Compton was a ragged tramp, tramping the roads, before he came here — "

"And all because he wouldn't cash a postal order for you!" grinned Skinner.

"Ha, ha, ha!"

There was an angry snort from Bolsover major.

"You needn't spin any more yarns about Compton, Bunter I've noticed that you've been sticking him for money, just as you did Mauleverer when he first came. The fellow was a fool to lend you anything, and it's just like you to turn on him and tell silly lies about him afterwards."

"Oh, really, Bolsover — "

"And unless you want a flogging from the Head you'd better not go around spreading such a fatheaded story," advised Bolsover major. "He might not think it so funny as we do."

"Chuck it, old man," advised Tom Brown.

"But it's true, I tell you!" hooted Bunter. "Honest Injun!"

"Ha, ha, ha!" The Removites in the Rag refused to take Billy Bunter seriously. They roared. In fact, that was how Bunter's story was received everywhere. Nobody believed him.

Harry Wharton & Co. roared as loud as anyone, but as Bunter persisted in stating that his story was true they began to see that the fat junior needed a salutory lesson.

"Ring off, Bunter," said Harry Wharton. "We've had enough of it. It's funny in a way, but it's not the sort of yarn any fellow likes to have spread about him. Chuck it, like a sensible chap, or you'll be getting yourself into trouble."

But William George Bunter would not "chuck it." Up and down the Remove he rolled, telling all and sundry that Richard Compton was a tramp, an imposter – a fraud. By which time the joke was getting a bit "thin." Thus it was not surprising that Harry Wharton & Co. brought the salutary lesson into effect.

William George Bunter was collared and held downwards over a study table, what time Bob Cherry administered "six" with a fives-bat. At every stroke Bunter's howls rang the whole length of the Remove passage.

"Now, old fat man," said Bob, breathing a little hard, "perhaps you'll forget that story and think of something else. If you don't, there's always another dose of the fives-bat waiting for you."

"Wow! Yow-ow! Beasts!" howled Bunter. "It—it is true, I tell you – I mean" – as Bob brandished the fives-bat – "that is to say it isn't! Yah!"

Harry Wharton and Frank Nugent were at prep in Study No. 1 when Dick came in. The new junior paused a little in the doorway, glancing at them, and then came firmly into the study.

What to expect he did not know. But he was assured that Bunter had told his story. There was no doubt about that.

What to do, what to say, if he were taxed with it, Dick did not know. He was passionately determined not to lie to fellows who liked and trusted him – he would have died sooner than that. Yet it was impossible to admit the truth – his promise and the commands of Sir Henry held him from that. For hours he had thought over the matter, keeping to himself in the secluded cloisters, but he had been unable to reach any decision. Now he had come in at last, not knowing what to expect, not knowing what to do.

Both the juniors looked up as their study-mate entered. Both of them smiled.

"Hallo! Where have you been all this time, Compton!" asked the captain of the Remove cheerily.

"I went out for a walk," answered Dick. "I've been loafing about since."

"You picked up trouble while you were out, to judge by the look of your nose," said Nugent.

Dick coloured, and passed his hand over his bruised nose.

"Yes. A rotten tramp – "

"My hat! You've been scrapping with a tramp?"

"Wingate of the Sixth came along and thrashed him," said Dick.

"Good old Wingate!"

"Well, there's news, old man," said Harry Wharton, smiling. "You don't seem to have heard it."

"News?" repeated Dick.

"Yes; and about you."

"About me?" Dick's voice was a little faint.

"Yes; dear old Bunter is going it again," said the captain of the Remove, laughing. "It seems that you've stopped lending him money."

"Yes."

"Time you did," remarked Frank Nugent. "You were an ass, Compton, to let that fat sponger plunder you so much."

"And now he's spinning a yarn," said Harry. "I'm telling

152

you because Bunter's told all the fellows, and it's a standing joke by this time. No need to get your rag out with Bunter. He's such a silly ass that it's not worth while taking any notice of his rot."

"Oh!" muttered Dick. "And what — what has he said?"

"That you were a tramp on the giddy road before you came to Greyfriars!" chuckled Wharton. "He makes out that he met you in rags and tatters in Compton Park — your grandfather's park. Ha, ha, ha!"

"Ha, ha, ha!"chuckled Nugent.

Dick looked at them.

He remembered how Wingate and Gwynne had derided the statement made by Pedlar Parker He realised that the Remove fellows were taking Bunter's tale in the same spirit. He realised, too, that that was what might have been expected, for even had a truthful fellow told such a story it was too steep to be easily believed. And Billy Bunter was well known for his amazing yarns. The true story was amazing to Dick himself, so amazing that sometimes it seemed like a dream. It was not likely to find believers in the Greyfriars Remove without very substantial proofs to back it up.

Bunter, of course, had no proofs to offer. He had only his word — which was never likely to be taken on the lightest subject. Certainly no one was likely to take Bunter's word in such a matter as this.

Wharton and Nugent were evidently entertained by the story. That was all.

Both of them were laughing, and they seeemed to expect Compton to laugh also.

Dick breathed hard.

He did not know whether to feel relieved or not. The thunderbolt had fallen, but it had missed fire. Bunter's story was laughed at — taken as a foolish and malicious invention of a fellow disappointed in his greed. In a few days it would be forgotten.

The secret, then, was safe.

But Ragged Dick was not sure that he felt relief. He was not called upon to deny the story. It was considered too absurd to need denial. It was simply laughed at.

That was a relief, and yet – Dick's troubled brow grew darker and more troubled.

Leaving these fellows – fellows who trusted him – in their false belief. Was that not tantamount to actual lying?

Was he not deceiving them?

"No need to get ratty, old man," said Harry, mistaking the gloomy expression on Dick's face. "Bunter's only a chattering ass. Nobody takes any notice of his yarns."

"He's not even worth kicking," said Nugent. "Let him rip, and he will forget it, and have a new yarn tomorrow about somebody else. I say, you're not waxy, are you?"

"Oh, no!" muttered Dick.

"Nobody believes a word of it, of course," said Harry. "Don't take any notice of it, Compton."

"I–I won't!" muttered Dick.

He turned to the bookshelf and sorted out his books for prep, glad to be able to turn his face away from his friends for the moment.

Wharton and Nugent exchanged a rather puzzled glance, and resumed their work, dropping the subject at once.

They had expected Compton to laugh with them over "Bunter's latest." He had struck them as a good-tempered fellow, easy-going almost to a fault. But if he was offended, there was an end of it, and the subject was done with.

Dick sat down to his work.

The three juniors worked in silence, Dick busy with thoughts that had little to do with the Latin he was preparing.

The danger had passed – he knew it. He need say nothing. Bunter could not harm him. He was not afraid of that. What troubled him was that the incident had brought home his position more clearly to his mind. At first, leaving everything obediently to the man who had rescued him from rags and poverty, he had seen no harm in coming to Greyfriars under the name of Compton – a name freely given him by the man who bore it. But more and more it was forced upon his mind that there was deception in it – that it savoured of trickery, if not actual imposture.

Why – why could not the old baronet let it be known that he was a Compton only by adoption? Why should the old man care whether it was known? Why could he not be allowed to tell these fellows the truth? Why must he be forced to listen to their frank, careless talk with a secret sense of shame, almost of guilt?

Silence in such circumstances came near to deceit, perilously near to it. And his tongue was tied. He could not fly in the face of the old baronet's commands – the commands of the man who had done so much for him, to whom he owed it that he was at Greyfriars at all. And there was the promise of strict silence that Sir Henry had exacted from him. It could not be right to break a promise.

But why, why did the grim old man hold him to a silence that was painful, almost guilty, and – so far as Dick could see – unnecessary and futile?

It was such reflections that brought the first misgiving into Dick's mind – a misgiving that all was not right in this strange affair – this miraculous change in his fortunes.

Could Sir Henry have had some motive unknown to him? Was it possible that he had some hidden, mysterious reason to fear the truth becoming known?

It seemed a wild thought; it seemed a wrong to the man who had saved him from rags and famine. Yet it lingered in Dick's mind; he could not wholly drive it away. Had there been some reason he could not imagine or even guess at for the old baronet's action – some purpose he had to serve by placing Ragged Dick in the position of the grandson who had died, and whose death, obviously, he must be keeping a secret? "Some sort of a swindle," Bunter had said, and the words haunted Dick. But was it possible to imagine the haughty master of Compton Hall concerned in any affair that was not honourable?

Dick went down to the Rag after prep with Wharton and Nugent, but he was not in a cheerful mood.

Bunter's tale was still a topic in the Rag, and the fellows laughed over it, and some of them jested with Compton; but they did not perceive that it was an unpalatable topic to him. As soon as that was noticed most of the Removites dropped the subject.

For the moment Ragged Dick's secret was safe!

CHAPTER 23

Parker Tries it On!

"**G**UV'NOR!"

Sir Henry Compton halted. His wrinkled old brown face contracted in a frown as he stared at the slinking figure before him.

Pedlar Parker touched his battered hat respectfully.

It required all Pedlar Parker's nerve to stop the haughty-looking old gentleman and address him at all. His manner was cringing as he stood abashed under Sir Henry's grim stare.

"Skuse me, guv'nor!" he whined.

"You rascal, what are you doing on my land?" asked Sir Henry harshly. "You are trespassing here! Take yourself off!"

"I got to speak to you, sir," said Parker. "It's important, sir, and when I come up to the 'ouse I was turned off by your servants, sir."

"I should say so!" exclaimed Sir Henry. "And if you do not get off my estate instantly, now, I will have you turned off by my keepers!"

"I got something to tell you, sir!" persisted Parker eagerly. "I've been watching for days, sir, for a chance to speak to you!"

"Nonsense!"

"It's true, sir — true as a die!"

"I never give to beggars, and certainly not to tramps!" said

157

Sir Henry. "You have nothing to expect from me but to be given into custody if you beg here! Take yourself off!"

"It's about that boy at the school, sir."

"What?"

"Him what you call your grandson, sir."

Sir Henry Compton started violently. For a moment the colour wavered in his face. It was a warm and sunny afternoon, but the old man was conscious of a sudden chill.

Pedlar Parker saw that he had made an impression, though he was far from guessing the thoughts in the baronet's mind.

"I know something about that young cove, sir!" he said eagerly. "He's a young rascal, he is, and I'm putting you on your guard, sir. I ain't asking for anything, sir – on my davy! Jest telling the truth about that young rascal Dick, sir."

Sir Henry pulled himself togther with an effort. It flashed into his mind at once that this was some associate of Ragged Dick's earlier days, who must have seen him now at Greyfriars.

"Are you speaking of my grandson – a boy at Greyfriars School?" he asked quietly.

"He ain't your grandson, sir."

"What do you mean – if you are not mad or drunk?" snapped the old man contemptuously.

"You've been took in, sir!" said Parker eagerly. "Took in and done, sir! 'Ow the young hound's worked it I don't know, but he ain't your grandson any more than he's mine, sir. His name's Dick – he ain't got any other name. Ragged Dick was what he was called by the coves on the road, sir – jest Ragged Dick and nothing else. I know him, sir – I know him!"

"Who are you?"

"Parker's my name, sir – Pedlar Parker."

Sir Henry understood. Ragged Dick had told him of the ruffianly tyrant from whom he had escaped the very day that the old man had found him in Compton Park. So this was the man!

158

"And why are you telling me this story, my man?" asked Sir Henry, still quietly.

"To put you wise, sir," said Parker. "Jest to open your eyes, sir. You're being took in, sir. 'Ow he's done it I dunno, but I know he ain't your grandson, 'cause why, he's Ragged Dick, the tramp, and so I know you've been took in somehow, sir, by a young swindler, sir. You look into it, and you'll find that it's so, sir, on my davy. You ask that young 'ound questions, and see if he can answer! Why, sir, I'd bring a dozen blokes that knowed him when he was tramping the roads – knowed him well, and could swear to him, if you wanted. He's took you in, sir."

Sir Henry eyed the man.

Knowing that the new boy at Greyfriars was Ragged Dick, Pedlar Parker knew that he could not possibly be, as was supposed, the grandson of Sir Henry Compton. The only theory he could form was that Dick had somehow made a foolish old man believe so. Certainly the grim old baronet did not look like a man to be easily imposed upon; but Parker knew what he knew – he knew that Ragged Dick was Ragged Dick!

Sir Henry smiled grimly.

"And you think I shall take any notice of this absurd story?" he asked harshly.

"You'd better, sir. I warn you you're being took in by a young swindler, sir!" urged Parker.

"Do I look like a man to be taken in?"

Parker did not answer that. He was, indeed, quite puzzled. The baronet looked like anything but a man to be taken in by an imposter.

"Do you think that I do not know my own grandson, a boy brought up under my own care?" said Sir Henry.

Parker eyed him in silence.

"You rascal!" said the baronet. "How dare you come to me with a foolish, lying tale like this? How dare you utter such a statement? By gad! I will have you taken into custody, and charged before the magistrates. I suppose you have begged from my grandson – is that it? – and he has treated you with the contempt such a ruffian deserves. And you have manufactured this childish slander. You shall repent it!"

Pedlar Parker backed away.

He was quite bewildered.

"I swear, sir – " he gasped hoarsely.

"Silence, you rascal!"

The ruffian stared at him. This was no foolish old man, taken in by a tale by an imposter; that was clear. Parker was a rascal, but he was no fool. It dawned upon his mind that if Sir Henry Compton regarded Ragged Dick as his grandson, it was because he chose so to regard him. Why he should so choose was a baffling mystery to the ruffian, a bewildering mystery. But the fact was clear. He knew now that Sir Henry knew the truth – knew that the boy at Greyfriars was Ragged Dick, once a tattered tramp; and he realised that Sir Henry was savagely enraged by the discovery that he – Pedlar Parker – knew it, too.

"You scoundrel!" said the baronet, in measured tones. "You slandering rascal! You do not know, perhaps, that you are talking to a magistrate! By gad, I will have you arrested and charged, and – "

"You're in it!" gasped Pedlar Parker. "I–I never knew that, sir. On my davy, I thought you was being took in, sir! I – Oh!"

The ruffian gave a loud howl as the baronet's arm went up, and his stick came down with an angry blow.

Pedlar Parker staggered under the lash.

"That for your lying tongue!" said Sir Henry grimly. "Now, go–go! If you are within ten miles of Compton Hall to-morrow I will have you arrested and sent to prison! Do you understand me, you scoundrel? Go!"

"By gum! I – "

160

Another lash from the old man's stick interrupted the ruffian. For a moment Pedlar Parker looked as if he would spring on the baronet; but the grim, fierce old face quelled him; he dared not. Muttering curses, he slunk away, and disappeared among the trees, burning with rage and disappointment and hatred.

Sir Henry Compton continued his walk, his hard face grimmer and harder. He had not foreseen this – that some outcast associate of Dick's early, wretched days might turn up. The possibility had existed, but he had not thought of it. But, after all, there was nothing to fear. Pedlar Parker was certain to clear out of the neighbourhood. He knew the power of a magistrate in dealing with a man of his character; he would not dare to linger. And if he told such a tale, who would heed or listen?

There was no danger.

CHAPTER 24

Light At Last!

" **H**ALLO, hallo, hallo!"

"I've seen that Johnny somewhere," said Harry Wharton.

Bob Cherry grinned.

"Relation of yours, Compton."

"What?"

Ragged Dick started, flushed and stared in the direction in which Bob was looking.

The Famous Five had walked over to Cliff House that afternoon, and they had taken Dick with them for tea with Marjorie & Co.

Dick had enjoyed his afternoon immensely.

Marjorie and Clara had seemed to like him; certainly he had liked them. There had been a pleasant tea, and a pleasant talk, in the school garden, under the shady old trees, and Dick had been in the best of spirits. It was more than a week since Billy Bunter had told his strange tale at Greyfriars, and that tale had been almost forgotten by this time. Even Bunter himself made no further reference to it, discouraged by the general disbelief and contempt of the Removites.

The danger had passed. It left no trace, save in the misgivings that it had brought into Dick's mind.

Under the westering sun the six juniors walked home from

162

Cliff House, sauntering cheerily by leafy lanes. And about half-way to Greyfriars they sighted a horseman, coming towards them at a walk up the shady lane.

Ragged Dick startled by Bob's words, fixed his eyes on the man, still in the distance.

He was well dressed in riding-clothes, mounted upon a handsome horse. Something familiar in his features struck Dick, though he was certain he had never seen the man before. The next moment he knew what the familiarity was— a resemblance to the hard face of Sir Henry Compton, though this was a much younger man.

"Your giddy relation, Compton," said Bob Cherry, with a grin. "Sort of an uncle three times removed, or something of the sort — what?"

"I suppose we'd better cap him, as he's one of C.... people," said Harry Wharton.

"The politefulness is the proper caper," remarked Hurree Jamset Ram Singh.

"Are you on speaking terms with him, Compton?" asked Nugent. "I've heard that your grandfather won't let him come up to the Hall. There's a lot of gossip about it in the neighbourhood, you know."

Dick nodded.

"Sir Henry has told me that he is a man of bad character, and that I am never to speak to him if we should meet," he said. "I—I think he has told the headmaster that if Mr. Roger should ever come to Greyfriars he is not to be allowed to see me."

"Quite right!" grunted Johnny Bull.

"I—I don't know much about him, of course," said Dick hesitatingly. Indeed, the waif had wondered a good deal at the old baronet's deep bitterness towards his kinsman.

"He's a bad hat," said Johnny Bull. "He's pretty well known in this locality — he generally turns up for the Courtfield races, and he has been fined at Courtfield police-court

163

for disorderly conduct. He's a thorough bad hat. I've seen him
drunk in a car with a racing gang."

"Oh!" said Dick.

"Don't pile it on, old man," said Bob. He's a relation of
Compton's, you know."

Johnny Bull grunted.

"All the better for Compton to know what he's like, so
that he can keep clear of him," he answered. "If the man had
any decency, he would play his blackguardly games somewhere else, where his relations don't live. He could back
horses and get squiffy at Newmarket or Doncaster, instead of
here. He's a thorough bad hat."

"He looks it!" remarked Nugent.

There was no doubt that Roger Compton looked his
His face had been handsome once, but it was
marked and bloated by riotous living and reckless self-indulgence. Harry Wharton & Co. regarded him with some curiosity
as he drew nearer. The reckless blackguard, a disgrace to an
ancient name, was well known in the locality, and his wild
doings were often the talk of the countryside. That he was on
the bitterest terms with the head of the family, that he found
a blackguardly satisfaction in disgracing Sir Henry's name in
the county where Sir Henry was a great magnate all the
countryside knew.

And all the more interest attached to the scapegrace,
because only the life of a boy – known to be in delicate
health – stood between him and succession to the title and
estates at the old baronet's death.

The horseman had observed the schoolboys, and his eyes—
puffy and blinking from late hours and strong drink – turned
upon them rather keenly. Ragged Dick dropped his eyes as
the man came nearer. This was Sir Henry's relative, his only
near relative, and his enemy. Dick had never seen him before,
but he could see reasons enough in the man's face for the
stern old gentleman's bitter dislike and scorn. From this man,

more than from any other, Sir Henry had bidden him keep secret the story of his adoption; if Roger Compton ever saw him, he was to believe, more than all others, that Dick was the baronet's own grandson. Dick had wondered why, without giving the matter much thought.

Having decided to "cap" the man, as he was a relation of Compton's. Harry Wharton & Co. raised their hats as he came up. Roger Compton pulled in his horse.

"You young fellows belong to Greyfriars – what?" he asked. His voice and manner were agreeable enough.

"Yes, Mr. Compton," answered Harry.

Dick's cheeks were burning. This man was no relative of his; yet he had to let the juniors believe that he was. Again that discomforting feeling of deception haunted and troubled him.

"A young relative of mine has been sent to your school recently, I hear," said Roger Compton. "Do you know him?"

"Yes," said Wharton, with a smile.

He wondered that Roger did not recognise the new junior; barred as he was at Compton Hall, he must have seen the baronet's grandson.

"The poor boy is in delicate health," said Roger. "I have been unable to call at the school to see him since he came back from abroad."

Harry Wharton & Co. contrived not to smile. They knew why the scapegrace had been unable to call at the school to see young Compton: because he would not have been permitted to see him. And they guessed that he was hanging about the neighbourhood now to catch sight of him outside the walls of the school.

Yet now that he was in his presence, he did not know him. It was odd enough.

"Is his health restored?" asked Roger. "I am naturally anxious to know."

"Oh, quite!" said Harry. "You'd never suppose that he'd

ever been delicate if you saw him now, Mr. Compton."

And Wharton could not help smiling now at the expression that came involuntarily over Roger Compton's face. Certainly, he did not want to hear that it was a "good life" that stood between him and the Compton succession.

"Then he is well now?" asked Roger.

"Quite."

"He never takes part in the school games, and so on?"

"Yes, rather; he's getting on famously."

Ragged Dick stood silent, looking at the ground. Roger Compton did not look at him, evidently unaware that this was the boy who went by the name of Compton at Greyfriars School. Harry Wharton & Co. did not feel called upon to enlighten him. As Compton had been forbidden by his grandfather to speak to the man, it was just as well.

"Impossible!" exclaimed Roger Compton, and he could no longer hide his annoyance and malice. "Impossible! He was a weak, puny lad – he was never expected to live. He could never have been anything but an invalid. You are not telling the truth!"

Wharton crimsoned.

"That's about enough!" he said. "Come on, you fellows!"

The juniors passed the rider, and walked on. Roger Compton stared after them, biting his lip with anger, and then he struck his horse a cruel blow with the whip, and galloped on up the lane, and disappeared.

Harry Wharton & Co. walked on towards Greyfriars, Dick still silent and with burning cheeks.

"Jolly odd that he never recognised you, Compton," said Johnny Bull. "I suppose you've changed a lot since you got well; that must be it."

"Blessed if anybody would think that Compton had ever been such a giddy invalid as that johnnie described," remarked Bob Cherry. "You've been jolly lucky to pull out of it, Compton."

Dick nodded without speaking.

"The dear man was awfully keen on getting information," chuckled Bob. "So concerned about his dear relative's state of health! He really is a bad hat, and no mistake. You could see by his face that he'd have been glad to hear that Compton was on his last legs."

"Plain enough, that," said Nugent.

Dick started.

"I thought so from his look," he said. "But why? Why should he want anybody to be in bad health?"

"Mean to say you don't know?" asked Bob.

"I can't imagine! He looks to me like a bad man," said Dick. "He looks like a very bad man, I think. But —"

"I fancy he's badder than you guess, then," said Bob, laughing. "Of course, as you've lived abroad" — Dick winced — "you haven't heard the cheery gossip that goes on round about here about your grandfather and his giddy relation. It's pretty well known that jolly old Roger is living on his expectations and the moneylenders; and with you in a roaring state of good health, how much money will they lend him on his prospects? I fancy it must have been a knock-down blow to him when he heard that you were well enough to be sent to Greyfriars."

Dick stared at him blankly.

"But why—why?" he panted. Back into his mind that haunting misgiving came, with a gleam of light — a gleam of understanding of Sir Henry Compton's motive.

"My dear chap," said Bob, in surprise. "You don't need me to tell you that that man comes next to you as heir of Compton Hall."

"Next to me!" muttered Dick faintly.

"Of course."

"He's rotter enough to think about that, and calculate on it," said Nugent, with a nod. "I rather think the money-lenders will dun him to death when they hear that Sir Henry's grandson isn't a giddy invalid any longer, but one of the heftiest chaps in the Greyfriars Remove."

"Ha, ha, ha!"

"Serve him jolly well right!" said Bob Cherry. "He's a bad hat! By gum, what's the matter with you, Compton? You look as white as a sheet, old man. Did it give you a shock meeting that bounder?"

"Yes," breathed Dick. "But—but I don't understand. I—I suppose Sir Henry can leave his estates to whom he pleases, can't he?"

"Well, my only hat!" ejaculated Bob Cherry in amazement. "I should have thought that giddy landed proprietors knew more about their own affairs than that! Mean to say you don't know that your grandfather's estate is entailed? Any kid in the village hereabouts could have told you that!"

"Entailed!" repeated Dick faintly.

"Of course."

"Oh!" muttered Dick.

He had heard of entail, though he had never thought about the matter.

"The jolly old estates, and the jolly old Hall, go to the heir male," grinned Bob. "No girls need apply! Besides, if the old gent could leave the estates by will, he couldn't leave the title."

"The—the title!" Poor Dick had never even thought about the title. He was thinking now.

"Don't bother your head about it, old man," said Harry Wharton. "It's common talk about here that Sir Henry's grandson was not expected to live, and that Roger Compton was up to the neck with moneylenders on his expectations. Serves him jolly well right to be let down! Don't bother your head about him. He's really a bad sort."

Dick nodded without speaking.

His brain was in whirl.

So that was it!

Bunter had surmised that it was "some sort of a swindle."
It was more than that. Roger Compton, rogue and blackguard
as he was, was the heir of Compton Hall; the baronet's grandson was dead! In the place of the boy who had died stood
Ragged Dick, barring the scapegrace from his inheritance!
That was Sir Henry's motive — the motive that the waif had
vainly tried to fathom! He was an unconscious party to a
fraud, a fraud for which the prison gates would open for him
if it became known. The hapless lad's brain whirled as he
tried to think of it.

He did not speak a word till the juniors reached the school.
Harry Wharton & Co., wondering a little, could only surmise
that the meeting with Roger Compton had given their chum
a shock, little dreaming how terrible the shock had been.

As soon as they reached Greyfriars Dick slipped away.

He shrank from meeting the crowd of fellows in the House;
he shrank even from the cheery company in the study. He
slipped away quietly to the solitary cloisters, to think, if he
could.

What was he to do?

Keep on the imposture — for he knew that it was an
imposture now! Cheat Roger Compton of his inheritance,
and thus become a worse rogue than the man himself was!
He could not, and he would not! Face the grim old baronet,
and tell him that he knew the truth — that he would give up
all he had received, and go back to hardship and want on the
roads; turn his back on Greyfriars, on the school he had
grown to love, the fellows with whom he had made friends —
all that made his young life worth living! If he hesitated, who
shall blame him?

CHAPTER 25

Ragged Dick Speaks Out!

SIR HENRY COMPTON removed the cigarette from his mouth and held it between two brown, lean fingers. His grizzled brows knitted.

He was seated on the bench in the little old summer-house in Compton Park. The little building was half-dismantled, overgrown with ivy and thick creepers, but it was a favourite resort of the old baronet when he was at the Hall. It was there that Ragged Dick had first seen him; it was there that Jenks, the keeper, had brought him the fatal telegram announcing the death of his grandson – the boy for whom he cared little, but in whom all his hopes had been centred.

The old man was thinking of it as he sat in the deep shade of branches and tangled ivy, through the interstices of which fugitive gleams of the sun came like gold on the sunny afternoon. He was thinking of it when he saw a boyish figure approaching through the trees of the park, and recognised Ragged Dick.

His grizzled old brows knitted darkly.

He had forbidden the boy to come, forbidden him to approach Compton Hall until Greyfriars should break up for the next holidays. Yet here he was – in defiance of the command. On Compton estate Sir Henry's word was law. Over his dependants, and even his tenants, he ruled like an

170

autocrat. On two thousand fertile acres he was monarch of all he surveyed. And this boy, whom he had snatched from rags and beggary, dared to dispute his will. Blacker and blacker his mastiff face grew as he watched the Greyfriars junior coming towards the summer-house.

Dick did not see him as yet.

He had gone up to the great house a little timidly. For two days he had wrestled with the problem of what he should do. Now his mind was made up. He had asked for Sir Henry, had been told that the master of the Hall was walking in the park. Leaving his bicycle, Dick had walked into the park to look for him, and, remembering how he had seen the old man sitting in the summer-house, smoking his incessant cigarettes, he turned his steps in that direction. He was determined to see Sir Henry before he went back to the school – if indeed he went back at all. On that point he was not decided.

It was in his thoughts to make a clean cut that very afternoon, to save the awkwardness of explanations to his friends, the pain of parting, by a sudden disappearance. Compton of the Remove would vanish from Greyfriars. Ragged Dick would tramp the dusty roads again, and that would be the end of this strange episode in his life. But he had to see the baronet first.

He came on, glancing about him under the trees for the tall figure of the lord of Compton Hall.

In the dusk of the summer-house the glimmer of Sir Henry's cigarette caught his eye, and he knew that the old man was there.

He stepped into the entrance, raising his straw hat, with its band in the Greyfriars colours, blue-and-white.

Sir Henry fixed his eyes upon the handsome face.

"You here, Richard?"

"I had to see you, sir."

"I ordered you not to come."

"I know."

Sir Henry breathed hard.

"Am I to expect disobedience from you, Richard — you?"

Ragged Dick flushed. There was a tone of scorn in the old man's voice. He realised, more clearly than he ever had realised, that to the haughty old gentleman he was still Ragged Dick, the tramp, serving a purpose, tolerated and patronised because he was serving a purpose, but still Ragged Dick, with no real claim on his patron.

"I am sorry, sir — " began Dick.

Sir Henry made a gesture with the lean brown hand that held the smoking cigarette.

"That will do, Richard! Go back to the school!"

"I must speak to you, sir."

"I do not desire to hear you," said Sir Henry.

"I must speak!" said Dick firmly.

The old man's face grew darker.

"Is this the beggar I picked off the roads?" he said harshly. "Do you presume to argue with me?"

"I have no choice."

"Silence — and go!"

Dick did not move.

He had not lost his awe of the grim old man, and he respected him in a way. But he did not go; he did not think of going. Matters had reached a point now when he had to be firm, and the old man was confronted by a will as determined as his own.

"If I go, sir," said Dick quietly, "I shall not go back to Greyfriars. I shall go back to the road."

Sir Henry laughed contemptuously.

"You will go back to rags and tatters?" he said. "I am not likely to believe that. Hold your foolish tongue, boy, and obey my commands and return to the school at once."

"I cannot!"

"What do you mean?" exclaimed the old man angrily. "Has anything happened at Greyfriars? You have not been mad enough to talk – to tell anyone – "

He broke off, with a savage frown at the boy.

"No, sir."

"Then go, and be silent still."

"I have told you that I cannot," said Dick. "I will leave you if you wish, sir. I cannot force you to listen to me. But if I go, I shall not return to the school; I warn you of that."

"What does this mean?" asked Sir Henry, after a short pause. "What have you to complain of, boy?" Is there anything you wish me to do for you, that I have left undone?"

"Nothing, sir. But I have found out something – I mean, something has become known to me, and I could not help it," said Dick. "I never understood why you had taken me up, given me your name, adopted me, as your grandson Richard was dead, and that you had given me his place. I believed that you had a right to do so if you chose."

"Do you question my right now?" exclaimed Sir Henry harshly, his eyes gleaming at the quiet, steady Greyfriars junior standing before him.

"Yes," said Dick. "I met Roger Compton some time ago, when walking with some of my friends in the Remove."

"I commanded you to hold no communication with Roger Compton, if he should seek you out."

"I did not speak to him – he did not know me. But, talking to my friends afterwards, I learned something."

"And what did you learn?" asked Sir Henry, with a sneer, but with an uneasy scrutiny of the boy's set face.

"That the Compton estate was entailed, that you could not legally leave it to an adopted grandson, and that if I became your heir, as you told me, it would be robbing Roger Compton," said Dick.

Sir Henry drew a deep breath.

It had been in his mind that sooner or later the boy must know.

The Comptons, of Compton Hall, filled a great space in the

countryside. Sir Henry was a great man, and his relative, the spendthrift, was the talk of the country; Compton affairs were a matter of incessant local gossip. Sooner or later his adopted grandson had to know. He was certain to hear enough, sooner or later, to set him on the track of the truth. It had happened sooner instead of later, that was all. But certainly he had not supposed that this ragged waif, saved from rags and tatters by his munifience, would dare to arraign him for what he had done; would risk losing a rich inheritance by uttering a word about what he might discover. Accustomed to his own way, to universal subservience to his lofty will in the little world where he reigned as master, the grim old man had never dreamed of opposition from – of all people – the waif who owed everything to him. He was discovering his mistake now.

"So you have learned this?" said Sir Henry at last.

"Yes," said Dick.

"And what then?"

"I—I suppose you believe that you have a right to do as you choose, sir," said the junior. "But I cannot be a party to it. I cannot. I know that Roger Compton is a bad man, a thorough rotter. But right is right, and law is law. He, and not I, is heir to the Compton estate, and I cannot cheat him. I am not your grandson, and I know now, only too clearly, that it was from no kindness to me that you called me so. I did not know that I was doing any harm when you sent me to Greyfriars under your name. I know now."

"Listen to me," said Sir Henry, subduing his anger and speaking calmly. "Roger Compton, my cousin, is a waster, a spendthrift, a gambler, a scoundrel. He is in the hands of the moneylenders up to the neck. He is the last of the Comptons, and therefore has the power to break the entail and scatter the estate. I have a very few years to live. At my death this scoundrel will be master of my estate, and it will be broken up to satisfy a crew of usurers. If anything is left over from their ravenous clutches, it will be wasted in disgraceful riot and extravagance. That I am determined to prevent. My grandson died – and I have taken you in his place. For you I care nothing – why should I care? For the Compton estate I care a great deal. You are the means of saving it from that scoundrel, and keeping it together. You understand? For this, I have taken you from rags and beggary; for this I exact from you implicit obedience. That is enough."

Dick listened quietly.

He could understand, and he could feel for the proud old man. But his resolution was unchanged.

"It is not enough, sir," he said quietly. "If Roger Compton wastes his inheritance, it will be his own to waste – it cannot be mine! It is not my business what you do, as long as you do not ask me to carry on a deception and a cheat. That I cannot do."

"You cannot? You, a beggar and a tramp!" said the old man savagely.

Dick winced.

"I was a tramp, but never a beggar, and never a thief," he said. "When I was with Pedlar Parker, I was beaten because I would not steal. And this – this is theft – "

"What!"

"If I step between Roger Compton and his inheritance, I am a thief, and I cannot and will not do it," said Ragged Dick. "I was bound to tell you so, sir, so that you will know what to do. You can throw me over if you choose, and let me go back to my rags. I have asked nothing of you, and I ask nothing now. But I cannot be a cheat."

"Gad!"

The old man raised his hand, as if he would strike at the handsome set face before him.

Dick did not flinch.

"I was bound to speak, sir," he said. "So long as you live, no harm is done, perhaps – Roger Compton has no claim in your lifetime. But after that, I could not step in and rob him. I could not, and will not. I could not let you believe that I would."

The old man was struggling with his anger. For some minutes he was silent.

"Listen," he said at last. "But for Roger Compton, there might have been another heir. I had a brother once – a brother much younger than myself. We became enemies, and it was Roger who first planted animosity between us – Roger who flattered my pride, and irritated me against my brother Robert – who caused at last the quarrel that led to our parting. We parted in anger. Robert went, and I never saw him again. He died in poverty and misery, and went to a pauper's grave. It was years later that I learned so. But for Roger Compton's treachery, it might never have happened, and Roger would not be the heir in entail to Compton Hall. My brother should have outlived me by twenty years. He should have left sons to carry on the old name, when my own line failed. Heaven knows, he may have left a son when he died, unknown to me, far away from me. But for his treachery and trickery, Roger would not now be my heir. Is he to receive my estate as a reward?"

Dick was silent.

He could not help thinking that the old man's grim pride and arrogance had probably been the cause of the bitter quarrel with his kinsman, as much as any treacherous intervention from Roger. But it was not for him to say so.

There was a long silence.

"We have said enough," said Sir Henry at last. "You will obey my wishes, my commands. There is no need to say more. Return to Greyfriars, and let me hear no more of this."

"I cannot, sir," said Dick. "I do not want to displease you or to disappoint you, but I must do what I know to be right."

"And this is the beggar I have saved from famine!" said the old man, with bitter scorn.

"I am ready to give up all that you have given me, sir," said Dick, in a trembling voice. "I would rather give it up – I ask nothing of you."

"It is too late! I cannot replace you, or I would send you back to your rags and tatters for your insolence," said the baronet harshly. "But the same trick cannot be played twice. You have appeared as my grandson, and now you must play out the game to the end."

"I cannot, sir. And even if I wished, I do not believe that it is possible," said Dick. "Roger Compton came to Grey-friars to-day. He asked the fellows to point me out, and he saw me playing football. I could see in his face that he suspected a trick."

"And why?"

"It is common knowledge that he saw your grandson a weak and dying invalid," said Dick. "He saw me as I am. Perhaps he does not guess, so far, that you concealed your grandson's death, abroad, that you took a nameless boy and called him your grandson. But he suspects something – I could see it. He has the right, and the power, to make investigations – to cause me to be questioned – and if I am questioned, can I tell lies, and lies, and lies? I cannot, and I will not. If my headmaster should question me, I am bound to tell him the truth – or nothing! And if I refuse to answer even, what will be thought of it?"

"And you learnt to be so particularly honourable tramping the roads and begging your bread?" said Sir Henry sarcastically.

"I never begged my bread – I have worked for it, and am ready to work again," said Ragged Dick. "I have starved, many a time, and will starve again before I will be a liar and a thief. If you were not blinded by pride and self-will, you would see that you are asking me to do what no decent fellow could do."

Sir Henry Compton started.

"You have forced me to speak plainly, sir. I am sorry to make you angry, but I do not fear your anger," said Ragged Dick steadily. "But I fear my own conscience, and I will not do what I know to be wrong."

Sir Henry Compton rose to his feet.

"Enough!" he said harshly. "More than enough! Go back to the school, and hold your tongue! I will think over this. I will think what is to be done. In the meantime, keep silent and play your part. As you have said yourself, until my death Roger Compton has no claim. You are not wronging him, as you call it, until you step into the estate at my death. My name and my bounty I have a right to give you if I choose – I may call you my grandson, if I do not make you my heir. Do you understand?"

Dick hesitated.

As clearly as if the old man had said so, he knew what was in Sir Henry's mind – that the longer the nameless waif enjoyed wealth and leisure, honour and distinction, the less likely he would be to give it all up for honour's sake when the time came.

But Ragged Dick had confidence in himself, and he felt that he had said enough.

"For the present, then!" he said at last.

"Go!"

And Ragged Dick went.

CHAPTER 26

The Mark of the Comptons!

"RICHARD!"

Ragged Dick halted, his brow darkening.

He was treading his way slowly among the beeches and oaks of Compton Park, on his way back to the house for his bicycle. The scent of a cigar came to his nostrils; he glanced round and saw Roger Compton.

The scapegrace nodded to him with a grin, as he called his name.

Dick walked on. The man's whole personality repelled him. In his rough days on the road Dick had come upon many a rascal, many a blackguard, but he had never met a man who impressed him as so wholly evil as Roger Compton. The man was bad through and through. Dick felt as if the touch of the blackguard's hand would have made him shudder. Looking at the hard, insolent, dissipated face, he almost thought that the baronet's scheme was justified — that any measures were justified to keep this scoundrel from ruining and wasting the land of his fathers.

Roger Compton swung out of his way and interposed, stopping the schoolboy.

"Hold on, Richard!"

Ragged Dick's eyes gleamed at him.

"Let me alone, Mr. Compton," he said. "I will not speak

179

to you. I will have nothing to do with you. Leave me alone."

Roger laughed.

"I want only a few words. You came here to see your grandfather, beause I saw you to-day at the school, what?"

"I came here for my own reasons."

"Because you saw that I suspected you?" said Roger Compton, staring hard at the schoolboy's face.

Dick smiled contemptuously.

He knew that the man's object was to startle him into an admission, a proof that Roger Compton suspected the trick that had been played. But the boy was on his guard.

Compton gritted his teeth, and his light bantering air dropped. He came closer to Dick, scanning his face savagely.

"You have some likeness to the Comptons," he said. "You have the Compton mouth — there is a likeness to the face. But there is no likeness to the puny weakling I saw two years ago — the wretched invalid who was at death's door even when he was sent to the South of France in the care of doctor's and nurses. You are not he."

Dick did not answer.

"It is a substitution — a trick!" said Roger savagely. "I suspected it when I first heard that Richard had returned to England — that he had been sent to school. Did old Sir Henry suppose me such a gull, then? If that sick lad had ever recovered, he would never have recovered to this extent. You young rascal, tell me the truth! Sir Henry's grandson is dead, and you have been put in his place to cheat me of my inheritance."

His eyes gleamed threateningly at Ragged Dick.

The Greyfriars junior's lip curled.

He would not deny the truth, but he would not answer the question. He would never cheat Roger Compton of what was his, but so long as the old baronet lived, nothing was his. So far, he had done no wrong. He never would do wrong. So far as he was concerned the Compton estate would go to the heir in entail. But it was not for Dick to betray the man who had befriended him — to place a weapon in the hands of this scoundrel. He stood silent, only his scornful look answering the angry scapegrace.

"Will you speak?" hissed Roger Compton.

"It is Sir Henry whom you should ask," said Ragged Dick sarcastically. "If you want information, go to him, not to me."

"Do you deny it?"

Dick shrugged his shoulders.

"Do you admit it, then?" hissed Roger.

"I deny and admit nothing," said Ragged Dick. "I only want to keep clear of you, Mr. Compton. Go and eat coke!"

"You young rascal! You are a party to a plot to cheat me — to rob me of what must come to me when that old fool is gone!"

"I am not a cheat, at least," said Ragged Dick quietly. "I shall never rob you of anything, Mr. Compton."

"Do you dare to tell me that you are Richard Compton, son of Sir Henry's son?" snarled Roger. "You — as healthy a lad as any Greyfriars — and he a puny, sickly boy whose arm was no thicker than your wrist? You lie, you young villian, you lie!"

"Have you finished?" said Ragged Dick coolly.

Roger breathed hard with fury.

"If you are Richard Compton, there is a proof of it," he said. "If you do not satisfy me, I will see what the law can do. I will not be cheated, I promise you. You call yourself Richard Compton, and if you are indeed he, changed out of all recognition, then there exists a proof. Bare your right arm to the shoulder."

Dick stared at him.

"What? And why?"

"Because if you are Richard Compton, you have the birthmark of the Comptons on your arm," said Roger. "It is a proof that no one could gainsay. I have seen it, with my own eyes, on the arm of Richard. If you are Richard, it is still there."

"There is a mark on my arm," said Dick.

He stared at the man in wonder as he spoke.

"A mark there may be, but not the one I speak of," said Roger. "If you are a Compton, you know the mark. Describe it to me."

Dick did not answer.

"I tell you that it is a sign of the race — that no Compton is born without that mark," said Roger. "Sir Henry has it, his son had it, and his grandson, and I myself. If you are Richard you have it, on your right arm near the shoulder. Let me see your arm, then, and I shall be satisfied. Refuse, and I shall not need to ask again whether you are an imposter."

"Well, I refuse!"

"That is enouh. I will satisfy myself, then!"

And with that Roger made a spring at the boy and grasped him.

"Let me go!" shouted Dick, struggling in his grasp.

"I will see your arm before I let you go," said Roger, between his teeth. "I will know the truth. If you are Richard Compton I am a ruined man; but I do not believe it, and I will know."

But the wastrel, though he was a man against a boy, was flabby from life-long indulgence. Drink and late hours had sapped his vitality. Ragged Dick was hard as nails — hard all through. He struggled fiercely with the blackguard, and suddenly he hooked his leg in Roger's, and sent the wastrel sprawling on the ground.

Roger spat out a curse as he sprawled, gasping.

Ragged Dick did not linger.

He had no desire for a brawl with Sir Henry's cousin on Sir Henry's land, and he was determined that the wastrel should never have the proof he demanded. The part he was playing had to end – he was resolved on that. But he was bound to consider the old baronet in the matter – to make things as easy as he could for the old man whom he was to disappoint so bitterly and completely. Roger Compton should learn nothing from him, at least.

While the gasping waster sprawled on the grass, Ragged Dick ran on, and in a few minutes was in the drive leading up to the great house.

Roger did not follow him.

Ten minutes later Dick wheeled out his machine and rode away to Greyfriars. Once, on the way, he glanced round, half-expecting to see Roger Compton again. But he saw nothing of the wastrel, and he reached the school and went up to Study No. 1 to tea, still Compton of the Remove for yet a little while.

*　　　*　　　*

"You here!"

Sir Henry Compton stood and looked down upon his cousin.

Roger had dragged himself up, gasping, breathless, spent by the brief struggle with the hardy Greyfriars boy. He was leaning against a tree, to recover his breath, still panting, when the old baronet came up. The tall, stern old man glowered down upon the panting waster.

"You here!" he repeated.

Roger gave him an evil look.

"I came to see you," he snarled. "I was refused admittance at your door, and I came – "

"I saw you attack my grandson," said Sir Henry coldly. "He dealt with you as you deserved, you ruffian. Now take yourself off my land before I call a keeper to remove you."

"I came to see you," repeated Roger. "I have something to tell you, Sir Henry Compton. I know your game."

"What do you mean, if you mean anything?" asked Sir Henry, his lip curling contemptuously.

"I know that the boy is not Richard Compton," said Roger, betwcen his teeth. "I know that he is not your grandson. I know, from this trick, that your grandson is dead, and that I am heir to Compton Hall."

"And what has put this wild idea into your mind?" asked Sir Henry, masking the icy chill of apprehension that seized him under an outward air of scornful indifference.

"You deny it, then?"

"I do not take the trouble. Tell such a story, if you choose," snapped Sir Henry. "Tell it where and when you like. Your character is rather too well known for any wild story you tell to be regarded."

Roger gritted his teeth.

"There exists a proof," he said.

"And that?"

"Richard Compton had the family birthmark on his arm," said Roger. "You saw me seize that boy. It was to force him to show me his arm. He refused; he dared not let me see it. If he is Richard, he has the mark of the hawk's head on his arm. If he is some nameless nobody whom you have substituted for your grandson, he has not the mark. Ah, that touches you, does it?"

The old man had blanched.

"It is a mark that cannot be counterfeited," sneered Roger. "The boy had never even heard of it, and he calls himself a Compton! He is a cheat and an imposter! He is no grandson of yours; he is no Compton at all, though he has some family likeness — a chance resemblance, for which you picked him out, I suppose."

"Is that all you have to say?"

"Will you call the boy and let him show me his arm?" said Roger. "I stand next as heir to estate and title, and I have a right to the truth. Call him, if you dare!"

"I refuse!"

Roger laughed mockingly.

"I knew that you would refuse. You dare not let the matter be put to the test, Sir Henry Compton. It is a plot — a scheme laid between you and this nameless young rascal to cheat me!"

"You believe so?" said the baronet, his grim old face unmoved.

"I know it — I know it!"

"If you know it, you need no information from me — no proof from the boy," said Sir Henry ironically. "Do as you choose in the matter. In the meantime, go!"

"I tell you — "

"Johnson!"

A man in gaiters was standing at a little distance, looking on, and he came up as the baronet called.

Sir Henry pointed to his kinsman.

"Johnson, see this man off my land. If you should find him on the estate again, see that he is given into custody for trespassing!"

"Yes, Sir Henry!"

Roger Compton clenched his hands.

"You—you dare!" he panted.

"Take him away," said the baronet coldly.

And, with the keeper's hand on his arm, Roger Compton was taken away, to be thrust out of the gates of Compton Hall.

CHAPTER 27

The Blow Falls!

HARRY WHARTON gave Dick a nod and a smile as he came into Study No. 1 in the Remove.

Dick was looking a little more like his old cheery self. Now that he had told Sir Henry Compton of his intentions a weight was off his mind.

For the present he had to continue to play his part. He was bound to consider his benefactor in every possible way. But his conscience was at ease now.

And with his conscience satisfied, there was no doubt that he was glad to keep on at Greyfriars.

He did not want to go; it was a struggle to make up his mind to go. Now that he had made it clear to the old baronet that he would not and could not carry on the imposture to the extent of wronging the rightful heir, there was no harm in what he was doing. He had a right to what the baronet had given him, if Sir Henry chose to give, and he was thinking now that he might finish up the term at Greyfriars, and leave when the school broke up — a few more weeks of happiness as a bright interlude in his clouded life.

So he smiled cheerily back to the captain of the Remove as he drew a chair to the tea-table. Tea was rather late in Study No. 1 that day.

"Jolly glad to see you looking so merry and bright

FRANK RICHARDS

Compton," remarked Harry Wharton. "I thought you looked
a bit down over that blackguard butting in to-day. I think Mr.
Quelch made it plain enough to him that he was to keep off
the grass, though. You won't see him any more."

Dick's face clouded for a moment.

"I hope not!" he said.

But he wondered.

Roger Compton knew – or at least, strongly suspected –
the truth; and he was not likely to let the matter pass.

What could he do?

As heir in entail to Compton Hall he must possess the legal
right and power to satisfy himself that a false heir had not
been subsituted to defraud him. But the old baronet would
resist investigation, that was assured. Legal proceedings were
costly, and Roger Compton was a ruined man. He had lived
and rioted for many years on money lent him at ruinous
interest by usurers, on his prospects – on the practical
certainty that poor little Richard would never live to inherit
from his grandfather. Were they likely to advance more
money when they heard that Richard Compton was restored
to health – that what they had already advanced to Roger
was as good as lost? If he told the moneylenders his story of
a substituted heir – yes, if they believed him, too! Otherwise, the cent-per-cent gentlemen would not throw good
money away after bad.

Dick realised that if he stood in with the old baronet,
determined to carry on the deception, Roger would have
little chance. The weakness of the position was that Dick was
determined not to be a party to a fraud – not to utter a
single falsehood. But Roger Compton could not know that –
could not dream of it. Undoubtely he believed that Dick was
heart and soul in the conspiracy, judging the boy by himself.

What could he do? What would he do?

The man was desperate, and he would not shrink from any
desperate measure. But what could he do?

187

Dick wondered, and the next day he more than half expected to hear something of Roger Compton.

But he heard nothing; and the next day, and the next, there was nothing, and gradually he dismissed the man from his mind.

It was probable that Roger had his mind fully occupied, at that time, in dealing with the usurers, disappointed of their gains and dunning him for money. He was not seen in the neighbourhood of Greyfriars School, and in a few more days Dick almost forgot his existence.

He had thrown himself into the football, and he was getting on splendidly, and Harry Wharton was already considering whether to give him a place in the team selected to meet Tom Merry & Co. of St. Jim's.

On the whole, now that he had made matters clear to Sir Henry, Ragged Dick was glad that the old man had not broken with him on the spot, as he had half expected and half hoped. This would be his only term at Greyfriars. Next term he would not come back when the school reassembled after the holidays. That would be the best way out of it. And in the meantime he was enjoying his school life immensely. Only the thought of the evil face of Roger Compton was like a dark cloud lingering on the horizon.

On the day that Tom Merry & Co. came over from St. Jim's for the match Dick found his name in the Remove team. It was sheer joy to him to find it there.

He turned out with the Remove team, and played a great game, fully justifying the captain of the Remove in giving him his chance.

Bob Cherry clapped him on the shoulder after the game.

"Gratters, old man!" said Bob cheerily. "Do you know you played best of the lot, excepting Wharton and Smithy? You're a rod in pickle for Rookwood!"

Dick smiled brightly.

It had been a glorious day, and a great game, and Ragged

Dick had enjoyed himself thoroughly. And he had the Rookwood match to look forward to now; he was sure to play at
Rookwood. Some of the Remove fellows went out with Tom
Merry & Co. in their motor-coach to the station, in the dusk,
and Dick went with them. But the brightness was to be
followed by shadow. As he walked back from Courtfield with
the Famous Five a man passed him on the road, and paused
for a moment to stare at him with evil, glinting eyes.

"Hallo, hallo, hallo! That's your giddy relation again," said
Bob Cherry, as he recognised Roger Compton.

Dick compressed his lips and hurried on. Roger Compton
interposed. The man had been drinking, and his face was
flushed, his step unsteady.

"Stop a minute!" he said thickly.

"Get out, you boozy bounder!" exclaimed Bob Cherry
in disgust. "You're not fit to speak to a decent fellow! Get
out of it!"

Roger did not heed him.

"So you are still keeping it up?" he said, with an evil stare
at Ragged Dick. "Still keeping up the cheat, you young
scoundrel and imposter? Do your friends know that you are
a cheat – living under a name that is not your own, substituted for a boy who is dead, to rob me of my inheritance?
Have you told them that?"

The next moment Roger Compton was sitting in a bed of
nettles by the road, unceremoniously shoved there by Bob
Cherry.

The juniors walked on; Roger did not follow.

They went in silence.

Dick's face was white as a sheet, his features set and rigid.
The blow had fallen!

Harry Wharton & Co. would have regarded the man's wild
words as the inconsequential talk of a drunken man and a
blackguard. But they had not forgotten Bunter's story,
though they had disregarded it. In spite of themselves, in

spite of their liking for Dick, and their faith in him, the scapegrace's words struck them with a chill of doubt.

It needed only a word from Dick to drive the doubt away. But that word he could not utter.

They expected him to speak, and he did not speak. In the evening dusk his face gleamed white.

The chums of the Remove exchanged uncomfortable glances; strange thoughts were in their minds. They walked on to the school, silent; not a word was uttered before they reached Greyfriars.

CHAPTER 28

The Story of Ragged Dick!

"**W**HARTON!"

Ragged Dick spoke in a low voice.

Prep was over in Study No. 1; scarcely a word had been spoken. Wharton and Nugent were troubled in mind. Dick was silent, miserable, conscience-stricken. They were his friends, and he had deceived them, and the deception could not go on. He felt at the end of his tether. It had seemed to him that there was no harm in playing his adopted part till the end of the term. So long as he was not questioned, so long as he told no lies, what did it matter by what name he was called – he, who had no name of his own?

But that meeting with Roger Compton had lifted the veil from his eyes. It could not go on now.

"Wharton!"

The captain of the Remove pushed away his books and glanced rather curiously at Dick.

"Coming down to the Rag?" he asked with an assumption of his usual cheery and friendly manner, a little awkwardly, however.

"I've something to say to you first."

"About what that blackguard said?"

"Yes."

Wharton paused for a moment.

191

"There's no need," he said at last. "The man had been drinking, and we know he's a rank outside. We believe in you, Compton – "

"Quite!" said Frank Nugent.

Dick smiled faintly.

"What he said was true," he answered.

"What?"

"Compton!"

The chums of the Remove stared blankly at Ragged Dick. They had wondered, and they had not known what to think; but his confession was like a thunderbolt to them.

"You're wandering in your mind, old chap," said Harry, after a long pause of amazement.

"It's true."

"Rot!" said Nugent uneasily.

"I'm bound to tell you," said Dick miserably. "I'd have told you before, only I was bound by a promise. But now that the man has told you, there can be no harm in my explaining – I'm bound to explain. I–I don't want you to think me a rogue, as that rascal does."

"I know you're not a rogue," said Harry. "But–but what are you saying, Compton? That yarn of Bunter's – "

"That was true!"

"But it's impossible!" exclaimed the captain of the Remove.

"I never denied it," said Dick. "You will remember that I never denied it. You fellows never asked me questions – if you had, I shouldn't have told you lies."

"Let's have this very clear," said Harry Wharton very quietly. "Billy Bunter told all the fellows that he'd seen you a few weeks before you came to Greyfriars – that you were a tattered tramp on the roads – that you owned up to it – that you were hanging about Compton Park as a trespasser. Nobody took any notice of Bunter's foolery – we all knew he was savage because you wouldn't let him plunder you."

"That's so. But it was true, all the same," said Ragged Dick, "and you fellows, too, had seen me in the same state, if you only knew it."

"We had?" exclaimed Nugent.

"Don't you remember, when I first came, you fancied you had seen me before somewhere?"

"Yes; but – "

"Well, you had seen me," said Dick. "Try to remember – one day near Compton Park, you found Pedlar Parker thrashing a ragged kid – and you chipped in, and he got away from the brute. I–I was that kid."

"You!" almost shouted Wharton.

"I!" said Dick.

"My hat!"

Wharton and Nugent gazed at the white face across the study table.

It was amazing enough, but they no longer doubted.

Now that they had the clue, they recognised Ragged Dick; indeed, they would have known him before, but for the apparent impossibility of any connection between Pedlar Parker's victim, and the wealthy grandson of the master of Compton Hall.

"But–but– " stammered Frank Nugent at last. "I–I can't understand. You were that kid – Ragged Dick – "

"I am Ragged Dick!"

"But you're Sir Henry Compton's grandson."

"I am nothing of the kind."

"But–but how – "

"Sir Henry found me in his park – that was after I met Bunter," said Dick wearily. "He had a telegram – I knew afterwards that it was a telegram announcing the death of his grandson Richard, who had died in a nursing-home abroad. He fell in a sort of fit, and I helped him. After that – the next day – he took me in his charge – he adopted me as his grandson, on the condition that I kept the adoption a secret. I saw no harm in it – you can fancy that I was glad of such a chance. I needn't go into details – that was how it came about. I saw no harm – I know you'll believe that – I thought he had a right to give me his name, if he chose, to make me his heir if he wanted to. But afterwards I knew – "

"He could not make you his heir," said Harry. "Everybody knows that the Compton estates are strictly entailed on the heirs male. And the title in any case would have to go to the heir by blood."

"I did not know it all then – I did not think about it. But when I knew – " Dick paused. "On the day Roger Compton came here, I went to see Sir Henry – I told him I knew the truth, and that it must end. That cleared my conscience – I had never meant to be a party in a fraud, and I was determined not to be. You believe that?"

"Of course," said Harry. "But then – "

"I should have gone then," said Dick. "It would have been better if I had gone then. But Sir Henry had placed me here as his grandson, and there was no fraud in the matter until he should die, and I should keep Roger Compton out of the estate. That I never meant to do – that I never would do. But Sir Henry has done very much for me – I felt that I had to let him down lightly, and I made up my mind to stay out the term here. I do not see that there was any harm in it. What Sir Henry gives me he has a right to give – and no one is harmed by my using the name of Compton."

"But what is your own name, then?" asked Nugent.

Dick shook his head.

"I don't know. I never had a name that I know of."

"By jove! But how – "

"But you must have some name," said Wharton blankly.

"I know! But I never knew it. I don't remember my father. I know he was very poor, and he died. I don't remember even his death. It must have happened when I was a very little kid. I believe he was tramping the roads when he died, and I was with him. Whether he had ever known anything better, I can't say. The first clear thing I remember is tramping with gipsy vans, and I believe the gipsies kept me after my father died, with their gang; but I was still a small kid when I ran away from the gipsies, and I've tramped the roads ever since – till Sir Henry Compton took me up. That's all I can tell you."

"And you never even went to school?" asked Frank in wonder.

"No. But at one time I tramped with a man who had been a master of arts at Oxford. He came down through drink; but he was a kind man, in his way, and he taught me a great deal. I was always keen on learning things – it turned out luckily for me when I came here."

"And you're no relation of the Comptons at all?"

"None."

"But there's a likeness," said Nugent. "You've got the Compton mouth, and the Compton brows, too. I've seen you looking just like old Sir Henry when you've been in a bad temper."

Dick laughed.

"That's fancy. I can't be like the Comptons when I've no connection with them in any way."

"I—I say, this is a jolly queer business," said Harry Wharton. "Does the Head know?"

"He thinks I am Richard Compton, grandson of Sir Henry. Naturally, he took Sir Henry's word for it."

"But dash it all, the old scout is dabbling in fraud, in playing a trick like this," said Harry. "If you succeeded him as the next baronet, as I suppose he intended, it's cheating Roger Compton out of his own."

"That was his intention, as I found out afterwards," said Dick. "He wants to keep that rotter from breaking up the estate and wasting it. Quite right, too, if it could be done by right means. I don't think Sir Henry realises that he is doing wrong. If the estate was not entailed, he could do as he liked with it; and he has simply shut the law of the entail out of his mind, and refused to consider it – that's how it seems to me. But I know what I must do."

Wharton took a deep breath.

"I'm glad you've told us this, Compton. I knew you were true blue; and I can't see that you've been to blame in any way, so long, of course, as you don't let the old man carry out his scheme. But what are you going to do now?"

Dick made a hopeless gesture.

"I don't know. I thought I'd stay on here till the end of the term, and then get out quietly when the school broke up. I'm bound to consider Sir Henry – I can't do as he wants, but I don't want to give him away and disgrace him, and cause a lot of gossip and scandal. It would be better for me to go quietly, without any fuss. But now that Roger Compton has brought the matter out in public, I don't know what to do."

"The man was drunk," said Nugent slowly. "If you dented the story, he wouldn't have a leg to stand on, and he would naturally expect you to deny it."

"But I can't."

"No, you can't," agreed Frank.

"I–I had to tell you fellows," went on Dick, after a pause. "I had to tell you something, and I couldn't tell you lies. But, of course, you won't say anything about it. I want to get out quietly, without any fuss or scandal – without giving Sir Henry more trouble than I can help. It's not long now till the end of the term, and, if you're still my friends, tell me what you think I ought to do."

"Of course we're still friends, fathead," said Nugent.

"Of course," said Harry.

"Then what do you think I had better do?"

There was a pause.

"I wouldn't do anything in a hurry," said the captain of the Remove at last. "While Sir Henry Compton lives you're not wronging anyone, and he's good for a good many years

yet. You're bound to consider him. It would cause a frightful lot of talk if it came out what he's done. He's done
wrong, that's true; but it's not for you to turn on him when
he's done so much for you. You're bound to keep the secret,
but yet – "

"And go at the end of the term," said Dick. "But if Roger
Compton should repeat what he did to-day – if there should
be more talk – "

Wharton rubbed his nose thoughtfully.

"He spoke to-day only before my friends," said Ragged
Dick. "But he may speak next time before others. He feels
certain now that there has been a trick, and he may think it
serves his purpose to cause gossip and suspicion. I–I don't
know whether I've a right to call myself a Greyfriars man,
but that sort of thing isn't wanted at Greyfriars. I can't
stay on."

Wharton nodded.

"You can't betray Sir Henry, and you can't stay on and
keep the secret without telling a bushel of lies as soon as
there's public talk about it," he said; "and you're not going
to begin telling lies, old man. No, you can't stick it out to
the end of the term if Roger Compton means mischief, and
I suppose he does."

"That was what I was thinking."

"But you'd better see your grandfather – I mean, Sir
Henry Compton – first," said Harry. "Warn him of what to
expect; and if he's got any sense, he'll take you away from
Greyfriars at once, before anything further happens. That's
the best way out. We'll be sorry to lose you, old chap; but
it can't go on like this."

Ragged Dick rose to his feet.

"That's settled," he said.

And, with a nod, he left the study. Harry Wharton and
Frank Nugent looked at one another.

"Poor old chap!" said Frank softly.

"It's hard on him," said Harry.

"That giddy old baronet must be a tough old customer. I can quite understand his being up against that rotter who is heir to his estate; but it's too thick. He's made use of that poor kid — made use of him unscrupulously — and made him accustomed to a lot of things he will have to give up now — things he'd never have missed if he'd never had them, but that he will miss now, poor chap. It's rotten hard lines. He could still do a lot for the kid if he liked, but I'm afraid he's more likely to throw him over."

"And what will become of him then?" asked Frank. "Back to the road — to the state he was in when we chipped in to stop that brute Pedlar Parker?"

Wharton knitted his brows.

"The old man's bound to prevent that, after taking the kid up," he said. "But if Compton is left on his own, I'll jolly well see that something is done for him. My uncle will take him in hand, I know, if I explain to him. He couldn't stay here after coming here in a false name; but there are other schools, and my uncle will help him out, if it comes to that. He jolly well shan't go back to rags and tatters!"

The next day Bob Cherry and Johnny Bull and Hurree Jamset Ram Singh were told. But the story remained the secret of the Famous Five. And all the five agreed that it was up to Dick to see the old baronet without delay, to warn him of what to expect, and then to withdraw at once from the false position in which Sir Henry Compton's strange scheme had placed him.

CHAPTER 29

The Last Word!

"**W**ELL?"

Sir Henry Compton snapped out the word.

He stood with his horse's reins looped over his arm; an old, gnarled, but still handsome and upright figure in riding-clothes. In a deep, leafy lane a mile from Greyfriars School, the old baronet had dismounted from his horse and waited – waited ten minutes or more till Ragged Dick came up from the direction of the school.

Dick raised his hat rather timidly to the old man. His face was flushed, but his manner quite resolute.

Sir Henry took no notice whatever of the salute. His deep-set eyes were fixed on the boy, gleaming under his grey old, wrinkled brows.

"Well?"

"You told me to meet you here, sir," faltered Dick.

Sir Henry made a gesture.

"I did not choose that you should come up to the Hall," he said. "If this arrangement is to end, if you are to betray me and fail me, the less you are seen there the better. I do not want the whole country to be talking of a fictitious grandson of mine, placed at a Public school, acknowledged in public by me, and vanishing from sight. I have my name and reputation to consider."

Dick felt a pang.

The old man had done wrong – hard and unscrupulous wrong – to carry out his daring project of keeping the Compton estate from the clutches of the spendthrift. But Dick could feel for his disappointment in the failure of his scheme. In his pride and arrogance, he had never dreamed that this tattered waif of the roads would dare to set himself up in opposition – that the nameless wanderer would venture to lay claim to a finer sense of honour than Sir Henry Compton, Baronet, of Compton Hall. It was a hard and unexpected blow for the proud old man, and Dick did not wonder that he was bitterly angry and disappointed.

"You insisted upon seeing me," went on Sir Henry. "As I did not answer your last letter, you telephoned to the Hall."

"I was bound to see you, sir."

"You are bound to be disrespectful, disobedient, and ungrateful," said the baronet. "I might have expected as much in a nameless beggar taken from the roads. I have made your fortune, and I am a fool for my pains. The wretched waif I have befriended is now setting up to teach me honesty and morality – to betray and threaten me. That is my reward."

Dick crimsoned.

"I do not mean that – anything like that!" he exclaimed. "I am grateful. It is hard enough for me to give up all that you have given me."

"But you will give it up?"

"I must," faltered Ragged Dick. "I told you in my letter – Roger Compton has told his story before a lot of Greyfriars chaps. How can I keep up the game after that? I had to tell my friends – I could not let them suspect me of being a liar and a cheat – but it is still a secret. Let me leave Greyfriars, sir, before I am bound to speak out to others who will not keep it all a secret."

"Roger Compton is helpless, if you play the game

thoroughly. His reputation is that of a villain, a liar, an envious scoundrel. Nobody would heed his wild accusation if you denied it."

"I cannot deny it."

Sir Henry made an angry gesture.

"Then if your headmaster, Dr. Locke, should hear that villain's story, and question you, you will tell him all?" he exclaimed.

"What can I tell him?" exclaimed Dick desperately. "I will be silent, if you choose, but silence will amount to an admission. I cannot tell him lies."

"Enough!" said Sir Henry harshly. "You have made up your mind to defy your benefactor. I realise now that you are in earnest, and that our connection must end. If you are to admit Roger Compton's story, you must not be at Greyfriars when it is told there. Now that he suspects the facts, the man has impudence enough to call on the headmaster and inform him of his suspicions."

Dick was silent. To the autocratic old baronet, any opposition to his lordly will was "impudence." Roger Compton was a bad man, a very bad man, yet he was entitled to defend his rights of inheritance, as Dick could see very clearly, though apparently Sir Henry could not. But the boy would not argue with the old man; it was useless to add fuel to the flame of his anger.

"The thing must end," said the baronet. "I understand that. I thought I had found a tool ready to my hand, and I was mistaken. I found a viper that would turn upon me and sting me. Let it end, then. Go back to your rags, since you prefer them – go back to hunger and want on the roads, if that is your choice."

"Better hunger and want, than lying and cheating!" exclaimed Dick, stung into retort for once.

Sir Henry knitted his brows.

"Silence, boy! You will listen to my instructions now,"

he said, "I do not choose to cause talk and scandal and comment — there has been more than enough of that concerning
my affairs. I would gladly remove you from the school to-day,
since it is clear that you will be of no further service to me,
and will prove a trouble and a danger instead. But I must
consider appearances. I shall communicate with Dr. Locke,
and ask him to let you come home for the week-end. You
will leave on Saturday as if you were simply coming to the
Hall for a few days. You understand?"

"Yes," muttered Dick.

"That will excite the least remark; and I shall think of a
reason for your not returning to Greyfriars afterwards. You
do not want me to explain to the headmaster that I have
imposed upon him a nameless tramp as my grandson?" asked
Sir Henry, with sardonic bitterness. "Your tender conscience
does not require me to go so far as that?"

"You will do as you think best, sir," said Dick, with a
heavy heart. "It isn't for me to dictate to you. Only I have a
right to say that I will not join in a deceit and a cheat."

"Enough! The matter is settled, then," said Sir Henry.
"You leave Greyfriars on Saturday — never to see it again!
I shall not, however, send you back to beggary — deeply as
you deserve it. I shall see that something is done for you.
You shall not starve."

Dick shook his head.

"I cannot do as you wanted, sir — and I cannot accept anything from you in charity," he said. "When I leave Greyfriars,
you will be done with me, and I hope you will forget that
you ever saw me. It seemed all the time too wonderful to
last; and when it is over I shall try to be content with what I
had before. I shall never forget what I owe you — the hap-
piest weeks of my life. But I shall take nothing more. I shall
clear off, and you will never see me again."

The baronet shrugged his shoulders.

"I have made the offer," he said. "It was due to myself to

make it. If you choose to refuse it, you are your own master, and I have nothing to say. You will return to Greyfriars now, to keep up appearances until the end of the week – I presume that I may depend upon you to that extent?"

"Yes, yes!"

"You will have the satisfaction, such as it is, of having disappointed and disobeyed a man who is not accustomed to disobedience," said the old baronet bitterly. "I have done less for others, and have received more thanks. To you, who had nothing, I gave everything; and you throw it in my face. You will repent it, you ungrateful boy; but your repentance will come too late to serve you."

"I don't think I shall repent it, sir," said Dick in a low voice. "I–I suppose you can't understand my motives. You have been too rich and proud all your life to understand that other people have wills of their own, and consciences of their own. You expect all the world to act like the menservants at the Hall."

The old man looked at him angrily; but his face relaxed again. Angry, disappointed, bitter as he was, there was something in the iron determination of this boy that appealed to his own grim obstinacy of character. Blinded as he was by pride and anger and prejudice, he realised what Ragged Dick was giving up for his conscience sake – he knew that it must have cost the boy a hard struggle.

"Let us not bandy words," said the old man in a gentler voice. "The matter is settled now; let us part."

"I–I'd like to say I'm sorry for having disappointed you, sir," said Dick. "It's hard to me to give up this new life, but it was harder still to make up my mind to disappoint you and overthrow your plans, sir. I'd like you to believe that. I'd do anything–anything I could – "

"You can do nothing," said Sir Henry. "But it is possible – if that troubles you – that the disappointment you have inflicted upon me may not be so great as you think. You have failed me; but Roger is not yet master of Compton Hall. I have not lost time since you came to warn me not to depend on you." He smiled sardonically. "I had a brother once – I told you of him. He died – in poverty, far away; but I had heard that he married in his poverty – a fool, as he always was. He wrote to me, to ask help for his boy – he had a boy – " The old man seemed to be speaking rather to himself than to Ragged Dick, standing silent, wondering. "That letter I threw into the fire, unanswered. My own son was living then, and he had a little son – the Compton line was safe. But now – now – if Robert's boy still lives, he may be found! It is twelve years since I heard of him, and Heaven knows what may have become of him – but he may live – and if he lives, he is heir of Compton Hall." He turned his eyes on Ragged Dick again. "If that child lives, I shall not need the help of a nameless waif to save my estate from Roger Compton. And since you came to me that day in the park, I have had detectives searching for traces of him – I will spend all my fortune to find him, if necessary; if only to leave him the entailed lands and the title. And if he is found – if he is found – "

Ragged Dick's heart beat.

"If he was found, you would need me no longer to keep up this imposture – and you would have thrown me over?" he exclaimed.

Sir Henry's lips curled.

"Do you dream that I would leave the Compton lands to a nameless stranger, if one of my own blood stood there to inherit?" he said contemptuously. "I must save them from Roger, but if Robert's boy lives, do you dream that I should prefer you to him? No – my pretended grandson would have disappeared – the farce would have ended."

"And that was what I had to expect, if I had done as you asked me, against my conscience and against my honour," said Ragged Dick bitterly. "You would have thrown me over if it suited you — as I should have deserved, too, if I had been such a rotter."

He checked himself, and turned away without another word. He heard Sir Henry Compton call to him, but did not look back.

The baronet shrugged his shoulders, and remounted his horse, and rode away slowly towards the Hall.

The farce, as he called it, was to end: On Saturday, Compton of the Remove would be known no more at Greyfriars. The pretended grandson would disappear — for ever; the baronet's hopes in the success of his scheme had turned to dust and ashes. Only a faint hope was left to him — the faint hope that after twelve years the orphan son of his estranged brother might be found. And upon that faint hope all the old man's thoughts were now centred, and he had no thought to waste on Ragged Dick.

CHAPTER 30

Harry Wharton & Co. to the Rescue!

" **H** ALLO, hallo, hallo!"

"What — "

"Look!" ejaculated Bob Cherry.

The Famous Five were sauntering along a leafy lane, in the direction taken by Ragged Dick when he had left the school. They had, in fact, walked out to meet him on his way back after his interview with Sir Henry.

In the distance, across a field, they sighted Compton of the Remove suddenly; walking slowly, his hands in his pockets, his eyes on the ground. He was about a hundred yards from them; and buried in thought, he did not see them across the intervening meadows. And suddenly, as Bob was glancing at the distant junior, two rough-looking figures leaped from a hedge, and rushed on Ragged Dick.

The attack was so sudden, so unexpected, that Ragged Dick was taken quite by surprise. He went down in the dust, in the grasp of the two roughs, fairly under the eyes of the Famous Five, staring across the fields.

Bob Cherry leaped across a ditch into the field.

"Come on!" he shouted.

"Put it on!" exclaimed Harry Wharton.

And the five juniors, running their hardest, fairly streaked across the meadows, towards the lane in which Ragged Dick was struggling in the grasp of his two assailants.

Ragged Dick was fighting hard, but he had no chance. He was down on his back in the dust, and a ruffianly knee was planted on his chest.

"Chuck it, kid!" said the man who was kneeling on him. "We ain't going to hurt you!"

Dick struggled.

"You're not going to rob me, either, you rotter!" he panted. "Help!"

"Quiet, you young fool!" growled the man. "We ain't arter your watch and chain. You ain't going to be 'urt, but you've got to come with us, see?"

"Bring him along, Ike!" said the other man impatiently.

Dick was dragged to his feet.

He was breathless and dazed by the sudden attack; and with a powerful rough grasping either arm, he was helpless.

"What do you want with me?" he panted.

"I tell you, you ain't going to be 'urt," said Ike surlily. "Nor you ain't going to be robbed. There's a gent wants to see you, and we're taking you to 'im, and that's all. We've been watching for you for more'n a week, and this 'ere is our first chance at you; and you can take it quiet, or you can 'ave a knock on the head, jest as you like; but you're coming!"

"Get him through the hedge, Ike."

Dick opened his mouth to shout for help, and a rough hand was clapped over it at once.

"No, you don't!" grinned Ike.

The two roughs dragged the Greyfriars junior towards a gap in the hawthorn hedge along the lane.

Dick still resisted, but he was helpless.

The words of the kidnapper had astonished him, but like a flash it came into his mind what the explanation was. It was Roger Compton who had set these two ruffians to seize him; and he knew why Roger wanted to see him – he remembered what the wastrel had said in Compton Park.

Richard – the boy who had died abroad – had the birth-mark of the Comptons on his arm. What that mark was, Dick did not know; but Roger, of course, knew it well; and he had taken this means of obtaining proof that Compton of the Greyfriars Remove was an imposter.

Ragged Dick panted and struggled.

The imposture was soon to end; but he had promised Sir Henry to keep up appearances till Saturday, and then to leave Greyfriars quietly, without talk or comment – to save the old man all he could. But Roger, with proof of the impos-ture in his hands, would not delay to strike. The exposure, the terrible scandal of a substituted heir and a lawless trick, would ring through Greyfriars – ring through the whole county.

It might even bring Sir Henry, lofty and proud as he was, within measurable distance of the law he had defied. It would place him, at least, to some extent, in the power of the scapegrace.

Dick fought hard for his liberty.

But the sinewy hands that grasped him were too strong for him; he was dragged through the gap in the hawthorns, into the adjoining meadow. Where the ruffians were taking him he did not know, but he guessed that Roger Compton was lurking not far away. And he was helpless.

But as the three came through the gap there was an un-expected happening. Five Greyfriars juniors, crossing the meadow at a desperate run, reached the gap in the hedge almost at the same moment. Ragged Dick had been dragged into the field that Harry Wharton & Co. were crossing to his rescue!

Crash!

Bob Cherry butted fairly into Ike as he came up, and the rough staggered and fell, releasing Ragged Dick as he did so.

"Oh!" gasped Ike.

"Oh, my hat!" panted Bob, as he rolled over the rough.

"Give 'em socks!" roared Johnny Bull.

"The sockfulness is terrific!" panted Hurree Jamset Ram Singh, as his dusky fist crashed into a stubbly face.

Ragged Dick dragged himself free.

"Help!" he gasped.

"We're here, old man – "

"Pile in!"

"Give 'em beans!"

Dick leaned on the hedge, panting. The Famous Five did not need his aid.

Ike and his comrade were being knocked right and left by the five sturdy juniors, yelling and cursing frantically; and in a couple of minutes the two roughs bolted back through the gap in the hedge, and took to their heels.

"Going – going – gone!" gasped Nugent.

"The gonefulness is terrific."

"All serene, old man?" asked Harry Wharton, turning to Ragged Dick. "Did they get anything from you? If so, we'll jolly well get after them."

"No!" gasped Dick.

"Good!"

"A pair of footpads, I suppose," said Frank Nugent.

"Well, they got more than they bargained for this time!" grinned Bob Cherry. "I've barked my knuckles on a jolly old nose! I'm sure the nose feels worse than my knuckles."

"Ha, ha, ha!"

"Lucky we came out to meet you, Compton," said the captain of the Remove. "You're not hurt?"

"No; only a bit winded!" gasped Dick. "It's all right! Thank you, you fellows, for chipping in."

"The second time we've had that giddy pleasure," chuckled Bob.

"Yes," said Dick, colouring a little.

"You've seen Sir Henry?" asked Wharton, as the juniors

turned back towards Greyfriars. The two roughs had vanished across the fields in the distance.

"Yes," said Dick.

"And it's all settled?"

"I go home on Saturday for the week-end, and don't come back," said Ragged Dick.

"That's the best way," agreed Harry. "But we're jolly sorry to be losing you, old man."

"The sorrowfulness is terrific," said Hurree Jamset Ram Singh, shaking his dusky head.

Dick smiled faintly.

"I'm sorry enough to be going," he said. "But it's the only way out."

And the chums of the Remove walked back to the school with thoughtful faces.

CHAPTER 31

Roger Compton's Last Card!

"**M**R. ROGER COMPTON!"

Dr. Locke frowned.

He made Trotter a sign to show the visitor into his study, but his frown deepened as the scapegrace entered.

Dr. Locke was a scholastic old gentleman, who lived and moved and had his being in books. But even into his scholastic seclusion something of Roger Compton's "juicy" reputation had penetrated. He had a profound contempt and dislike for the shady, disolute, blackguardly man who was a disgrace to his old name, and he was very far from pleased to see him.

He rose and fixed his eyes on the man, disregarding the hand Roger held out to him.

Roger shrugged his shoulders as he let the disregarded hand fall to his side again.

"This is unexpected – very unexpected, sir!" said Dr. Locke icily. "I must ask you to be brief, Mr. Compton. I can imagine no reason why you should call upon me."

"The pleasure of seeing you, sir, is not my only reason," said Roger sarcastically.

"Quite so. If you have any business here, kindly state it."

"I have a young relative in this school – "

Dr. Locke raised his hand.

"If you desire to see him — "

"I do."

"Your desire cannot be acceded to. I have the very strict instructions of Sir Henry Compton that you are never to see or to address his grandson," said Dr. Locke. "These instructions have my own full approval. Your reputation is known to me, Mr. Compton."

"My reputation, whatever it may be, is not Sir Henry's only reason," said Roger, with a sneer.

"I have nothing to do with your family feuds, sir."

"The family feud is not the only reason, either. I presume, Dr. Locke, that you do not desire a scandal that would make the name of Greyfriars sing through the whole country — with your own name as a possible partner in a lawless conspiracy?"

Dr. Locke stared at him. His impression was that Roger Compton had been drinking.

"Calm yourself, Mr. Compton. I must warn you that if you make a scene here you will regret it," he said.

"I am not here to make a scene, Dr. Locke. I am here to make an inquiry which I have every right to make. Will you hear me?"

"You may proceed."

"You have received a boy into this school under the name of Richard Compton, of Compton Hall," said Roger. "You may have heard that young Richard was an invalid from birth, that his life was despaired of, that he lived for years in a nursing-home in the South of France — "

"I have heard all this."

"You cannot fail to have been surprised by his apparent restoration to perfect health.

"Surprised and pleased, sir."

"Pleased, no doubt, from your benevolent heart," said the scapegrace. "But in the circumstances you will scarcely expect me to be pleased, as the boy stands between me and the finest estate in Kent."

"I cannot discuss any such base considerations, Mr. Compton. I am surprised that even you should refer to such things."

"Let me explain. I have reason — good reason — to believe that Sir Henry's grandson died in the nursing-home in France, and that the death was concealed — "

"Sir Henry's grandson is now at Greyfriars, in the Lower Fourth Form," said the Head, with a stare of amazement.

"That is the point in dispute, sir. I dispute the boy's identity. I suspect — I have reason to suspect — that the boy Richard died abroad, and that Sir Henry substituted another in his place to keep me out of my inheritance."

"Absurd!"

"You cannot credit it?" sneered Roger.

"Not for a single instant."

"And what if I can prove it?"

"Nonsense!" said Dr. Locke disdainfully. "Mr. Compton, I am wasting time in listening to such a wild story, and my time is of value."

"I will go, Dr. Locke, if you choose, but I shall return, accompanied by a solicitor, possibly by a police-constable," said Roger Compton. "It is for you to decide whether you will have a scene. I ask to be allowed to see the boy — in your presence, and in the presence of his Form-master, if you wish. I will tell you why. Richard, if he lives, bears the birth-mark of the Comptons, a hawk's head, on his arm. I saw it in his infancy. His grandfather would not dare deny it. His nurses can be produced to swear to it, his doctor, servants — many people. The fact is established beyond doubt."

"What of it?"

"Let it be proved that this boy, whom you know as Richard Compton, bears that mark on his arm."

"Undoubtedly he does, if it is as you say," said Dr. Locke.

"Let it be seen, then," sneered the scapegrace. "Let me see

it, and I will apologise to you, Dr. Locke, for wasting your valuable time; I will leave this place and never seek to see the boy again. If he is Richard Compton I have a right to know it – "

"He is Richard Compton."

"I have a right to the proof. Listen, sir! If he is the genuine heir of Compton Hall I am a ruined man. Sir Henry is my enemy, but if this boy is his grandson I can only beg from that hard old man money to help me flee across the seas to escape from my creditors. I make no secret of my position. For years I have lived on my expectations. The boy was never expected to live, and the usurers advanced me money. I am in debt so deep that when I come into the estate I must break the entail and sell almost all the lands, even the old house. All this I have had, and spent, because the boy could not have lived. Can you imagine the feelings of the greedy moneylenders whose money I have spent when they know that not a shilling can be repaid?"

Roger's voice was husky and thick.

"Can you imagine it?" he rasped out. "Well, if this boy is the genuine heir, I am so thoroughly ruined that I must flee from England, lucky if I even escape with my freedom. Do you understand? I must beg help from Sir Henry to enable me to run. But I do not believe that he is the true heir. I am assured that he is a substituted cheat. Let the matter be tested, here and now."

Dr. Locke hesitated.

The man's almost savage earnestness impressed him.

"If you refuse," went on Roger, "I am not powerless. I will spread far and wide my story of this cheat and imposture; I will gain legal powers to force an examination of the boy, as I would have done already had I not been crippled by want of money. But I will not be cheated of an estate. If you prefer trouble, and scandal, and disgrace, have your way; if you desire to see justice done, and to see the last

214

of me, let the boy be called here and the Compton birthmark displayed in my sight. I repeat that if he has the hawk's head of the Comptons on his arm I shall cross the sea to-morrow morning, and never see England again."

Roger's eyes glittered at the Head.

"It shall be so, then," said the Head. "Your story is false and absurd — the imaginings of a wicked and disappointed man, I am assured of that. But if the proof is so easy to come by, you shall have it."

Dr. Locke rang his bell.

A minute later Trotter was sent to Mr. Quelch with the request that the Remove master would bring Compton of the Lower Fourth to the headmaster's study.

Roger Compton sat down to wait, a grin of anticipated triumph on his face. And the Head of Greyfriars, watching the cunning, evil, triumphant face, felt a throb of doubt.

CHAPTER 32

The Proof!

"**C**OMPTON!"

"Hallo, hallo, hallo! Compton!"

Ragged Dick looked round.

He was strolling in the quadrangle with Harry Wharton, after classes, when Bob Cherry hailed him from the direction of the House.

"Wanted, old man!" bawled Bob.

"Right-ho!"

"Quelchy wants you," said Bob, as Compton ran up. "Cut into the House. It's all right, I think — not a licking!"

Dick nodded and smiled, and ran into the House. Mr. Quelch was waiting for him there. He gave the boy a kind smile.

"Dr. Locke desires to see you, Compton," he said. "You will come with me to his study."

"Yes, sir," answered Dick.

He followed the Remove master down the long, wide corridor.

It did not even cross his mind whom he was to meet in the Head's study. It was Friday afternoon — his last day at Greyfriars, though so far only his friends knew that. On the morrow he was to go. He was thinking of that, and certainly he was not thinking of Roger Compton.

He followed the Remove master into the Head's study, and then he saw the scapegrace.

He started back a little.

Roger rose to his feet and fixed his evil, mocking eyes on the boy.

"This is the boy," he said.

"This is Sir Henry Compton's grandson!" said Dr. Locke coldly.

"That is what we shall prove. What does the boy himself say?" sneered Roger. "Has he learned his lesson so well as to lie without faltering? Boy, answer me! How long have you been called by the name of Compton?"

Ragged Dick looked at him steadily.

"I will not answer you, or speak to you, Mr. Compton," he said.

"You insolent young scoundrel!"

"Silence, sir!" exclaimed the Head sharply. "Compton is quite right. His grandfather has forbidden him to speak to you, and rightly so."

Roger gritted his teeth.

"I care nothing for that. Let him be silent if he chooses, but let me see the birthmark — if it exists."

Ragged Dick's heart almost stopped beating.

It had come to this, then! That ruffianly attempt to seize him in the fields and search him for the Compton mark had failed, owing to the prompt aid of the Famous Five. But Harry Wharton & Co. could not help him now.

He backed away, his face paling.

The evil grin of the scapegrace followed him.

"He is afraid of the test!" grinned Roger.

"Compton, you have nothing to fear," said the Head gently. "This man will not be allowed to interfere with you in any way. You are under your headmaster's protection."

"Thank you, sir," muttered Dick.

"This man — a relative of yours — has some wild belief

that you are not in truth the grandson of Sir Henry Compton," went on the Head. "The idea is absurd – ridiculous! I know it, my boy!"

"Absurd indeed!" exclaimed Mr. Quelch.

Dick did not speak.

"But as it happens, he stands next in succession to the estates, and he threatens to cause a public investigation of his preposterous theory – he may or may not have the power to carry out his threat, but it is unnecessary that the matter should go so far," said Dr. Locke. "He states that a well-known birthmark exists on Richard Compton's arm – sufficient proof of his identity. He professes that he will be satisfied if he sees it. For the sake of ending his absurd suspicions, and closing a very unpleasant incident, Compton, I desire you to show your relative your arm, and thus satisfy him."

Dick did not move.

On the morrow all would have been well; the gates of Greyfriars would have closed behind him for ever. The scheme would have been at an end. Sir Henry, disappointed, would at least have been saved from exposure as a deceiver and a trickster. But now –

"You hear me, Compton?" said the Head, raising his eyebrows a little.

"Yes, sir!" faltered Dick.

"Then do as I tell you!"

Slowly Dick peeled off the well-fitting jacket.

"On what part of the arm is the mark, Mr. Compton?"

"Between the elbow and the shoulder – if it exists!"

"Roll up your sleeve, Compton, to the shoulder."

Dick did not stir.

Roger chuckled like a triumphant gnome.

"I will help him!" he grinned.

He strode towards the boy and grasped him. Ragged Dick would have thrust him back, but the wastrel grasped him savagely, and with a wrench tore the shirt-sleeve from wrist to shoulder. The white, muscular arm of the junior was revealed.

Roger stared at it – and staggered back with a furious oath. His face was white with rage and dismay.

"The birthmark!" he hissed. "The mark of the Comptons!"

Dark, on the white skin, was a strange mark, in shape like the head of a hawk. It was obviously a birthmark, and if it was a mark familiar to the eyes of Roger, it was a dumbfounding discovery to Ragged Dick.

He staggered against the wall, scarcely breathing. What did it mean – what could it mean?

Roger, in his rage and despair, struck his own forehead with his clenched fist.

"The game's up! A thousand curses on – "

"Silence, sir!" exclaimed the Head indignantly. "You have found, it seems, the birthmark you looked for, which proves that this boy is a Compton! You admit the falsity of your absurd suspicions! Silence, sir, and go!"

And, with a curse on his lips, Roger Compton went.

The Head gave Dick a kind glance.

"You may put on your jacket, Compton. You may go, my boy!"

Silently, dazedly, Ragged Dick obeyed.

He went down the corridor like a fellow in a dream. The mark of the Comptons – the unmistakable sign of the Compton race – so unmistakable that it had convinced the evil, suspicious Roger – and he bore it, and had borne it from his birth! What could it mean? Who was Ragged Dick?

CHAPTER 33

The Rightful Heir!

" IT'S the last time – help me to go; give me a hundred pounds to escape! I give in – I give in!"

Sir Henry Compton stared at the cringing wretch before him, hard, cold, disdainful, but deeply surprised. Roger Compton looked like the wreck of himself; the sudden breaking of all his hopes had overwhelmed him. The dissolute, impudent adventurer had turned into the cringing wretch begging for alms, to flee and escape from hungry creditors, perhaps from worse. The crash he had long staved off, while he waited and hoped for the death of the boy Richard, had come at last, and the scapegrace was a broken man.

"And what does this mean?" said Sir Henry grimly, sardonically. "The last time I saw you, you threatened me – "

"I believed it then," panted Roger wretchedly. "I believed that you had substituted a cheat for a dead grandson – I was sure of it! I believed it – I knew you capable of it."

"And you know now that the boy is Richard?"

"Yes, yes."

Sir Henry gazed at him hard.

"And you have come to me with this lie on your lips, for a hundred pounds?" he said with bitter contempt.

"I tell you I've put it to the test," said Roger. "I swear I believed that he was a substitute – I swear it. I never dreamed that the Compton mark would be found on his arm. It could not be counterfeited, and I made him show me his arm in the presence of his headmaster."

Sir Henry started violently.

"What? Then you saw – "

"I saw the birthmark!" groaned Roger. "I never dreamed to see it – I believed that he was a cheat! But it was there – and I'm beaten!"

Sir Henry's face was almost convulsed.

"Are you mad, or is this a trick?" he shouted. "You dare to tell me that you saw the Compton mark on that boy's arm?"

"With my own eyes."

"Great Heaven!"

Sir Henry leaned almost feebly against the great mantelpiece. His eyes were fixed on the cringing figure before him. There was no doubting Roger's earnestness, his terrified earnestness. He was a man broken, thinking only of flight before flight was too late to save him. And it was because he had seen the hereditary mark of the Comptons on the arm of Ragged Dick, the nameless, tattered waif of the roads.

Who, then, was the boy?

Like a glimmer of light it came into the old man's mind. He was a Compton, then – in the veins of this tattered lad whom he had snatched from the roads, ran the blood of his ancient race. He was a Compton, and there was only one Compton whom he could be – the lost untraced son of Robert Compton – nephew of the old man who, all unknowingly, had adopted him as grandson! Dick – Ragged Dick – the nameless waif – was the rightful heir of Compton Hall – what Sir Henry had falsely called him, he was in sober truth!

Ignorant of the strange, disturbing thoughts working in the old baronet's mind, Roger gazed at him, cringing, fearful.

Will you help me to get clear? It's the last time – the last time – "

"Enough! You shall have the money – and go! If what you have told me is true, you shall have ten times what you have asked! Wait!"

Sir Henry strode from the room.

Five minutes later he was riding for Greyfriars, as fast as his swiftest horse could gallop – to see Ragged Dick – his nephew!

*　　　　*　　　　*

It was more than a nine days' wonder at Greyfriars.

Ragged Dick left that Saturday; but for long, long afterwards his strange tale was talked of in the studies.

A stranger tale was seldom told.

Nephew of Sir Henry Compton, heir of Compton Hall – the junior who had been called the old baronet's grandson! It was a strange enough tale, but a true one. For a long time there was investigation; the little that Dick was able to tell of his early life helped in the final tracing of Robert Compton, the tracing of Dick's father, who had died in want, refused help by the brother who had cast him off.

Roger Compton, skulking in a foreign country from creditors and detectives, heard the story, learned that the old baronet's nephew was recognised, installed at the Hall as heir to title and estates, and gritted his teeth with rage as he heard it – realising the part that he had unwittingly played in the discovery that had ended all his hopes.

Dick did not return to Greyfriars – there had been too much comment on the strange story, and it was considered better not. With his newly-found uncle, he left to travel abroad for a year – after that it was possible that Greyfriars would see him again.

But whether they saw him again or not, his friends there were not likely to forget "Ragged Dick."

THE END